THE CHINA FACTORY

Mary Costello grew up in County Galway. Her collection of short stories, *The China Factory* (2012), was nominated for the Guardian First Book Award. Her debut novel, *Academy Street* (2014), was the winner of Irish Book of the Year Award and was shortlisted for the Costa First Novel Award. She lives in Dublin.

D0913444

Also by Mary Costello

Academy Street

THE CHINA FACTORY

MARY COSTELLO

CANONGATE
Edinburgh · London

This paperback edition published in Great Britain in 2015 by
Canongate Books Ltd.
14 High Street
Edinburgh
EH1 1TE

www.canongate.tv

1

Copyright © Mary Costello, 2012

The moral right of the author has been asserted

First published in 2012 by Stinging Fly Press, PO Box 6016, Dublin 1

Earlier versions of some of these stories appeared in
The Sunday Tribune, The Hennessy Book of Irish Fiction
and in *The Stinging Fly*

The author and Canongate Books gratefully acknowledge the financial support
of The Arts Council Ireland/An Chomhairle Ealaíon

British Library Cataloguing-in-Publication Data
A catalogue record for this book is available on
request from the British Library

ISBN 978 1 78211 601 1

Set in Palatino

Printed and bound in Great Britain by Clays Ltd., St Ives plc

Contents

The China Factory   5

You Fill Up My Senses   21

Things I See   33

The Patio Man   45

This Falling Sickness   55

Sleeping With A Stranger   67

And Who Will Pay Charon?   79

The Astral Plane   91

Little Disturbances   107

Room In Her Head   121

Insomniac   133

The Sewing Room   141

THE CHINA
FACTORY

And night by night, down into solitude,
the heavy earth falls far from every star.

We are all falling. This hand's falling too—
all have this falling-sickness none withstands.

RAINER MARIA RILKE

THE CHINA FACTORY

The summer I turned seventeen I worked as a sponger in a china factory. I walked to the end of our road every morning to catch my lift to the city with Gus Meehan, and every evening I came home with a film of fine dust lodged in the pores of my skin. From the back seat I had a view of Gus's broad shoulders and the china clay caked in the creases of his neck and in his grey hair. The air inside the car smelled of cigarette ash and stale masculine sweat. Gus's other passenger, Martha Glynn, was a woman in her thirties from his end of the parish, and was engaged to be married to a local man for over twelve years. Martha worked in the office of an electronics factory in the industrial estate. Gus was shy and deferential to everyone but more so to Martha, sitting beside him in her good skirt and white blouse. He had a slight stammer and drew his meaty hands close to him on the steering wheel, as if they might cause offence.

The spongers' station was at the lower end of the factory between the moulding area and the kilns, close to the yard entrance. All day long I stood in my white coat at a wooden table, first paring, then dampening and sponging off the symmetry lines that the moulds left on the clay cups. The cups were cool and damp to the touch, and brittle enough to collapse at the slightest pressure. My hands, dipping in water for hours, were pale and crinkled and spotless by evening. All day long the radio churned out the pop hits of that summer and the sun spilled in through skylights and fell in yellow pools on the factory floor. I would sigh and think of home and the farm work and when the thoughts grew lonesome and a small ache began to surface, I would carry my basin over to the big steel sink near the entrance and spill out the cloudy white water. I smiled when I passed the other girls those first days, and longed to speak, but feared that words would betray the yearning for friendship that I felt inside.

Gus was the only soul I knew in the china factory at the start. We parted in the car park on my first morning and I caught sight of him later on in heavy boots and dirty white overalls, rolled down and knotted at his waist. He lurched in from the yard, leaning forward as he hauled a wagon laden with bags of clay. His face glistened with sweat. When he passed the sinks and the sponging tables, dragging his wagon like a beast of burden, he did not raise his head or look for me. He did not seem to be the same Gus I'd known that morning.

That summer was hot. The kilns fired all day long, burning the air dry, irritating our skin and leaving us hot and cross and exhausted. Further up the factory the cups and plates and vases were transformed into white glazed china and further along again they were decorated with flowers and Celtic designs and gold-leaf rims. The girls in the art and admin departments floated in and out through a white door at the far end that led to the elegant showrooms, with their high ceilings and antique furniture and chandeliers.

At lunch time every day we clocked out and walked down the curved driveway and up to the shops at Mervue for Snack bars, Coke, cigarettes. The first few days—before I knew better—I sat alone in the dank basement canteen and bought a 7-Up and ate the sandwich I'd brought from home. The quietness amplified my isolation and after two days the smell of dirty oilcloths drove me outside. I sat under a tree and read a book. The lawn was wide, perfectly mown, with old oak trees along the high wall, and shrubs and flowers in the borders. The driveway curved up from the gate and then split, with one fork leading round the back to the factory and the other to the main house and Visitors' Centre at the front. The house was Georgian with rows of high paned windows and pillars and granite steps up to the front door. Inside, the hall was carpeted in deep navy blue. Day trippers and coach loads of Americans arrived each day and traipsed through the showrooms in search of dinner services and cake stands and wall plates.

When the other girls returned from Mervue they dropped onto the grass beside me and lit up their cigarettes. They were older than me, harder, funnier and more robust in their dealings with each other than I was accustomed to.

'I'd never go all the way with Francis,' Marion said.

Marion was the senior sponger and the self-appointed leader, the one who complained to the supervisor about the heat or the infrequency of our toilet and cigarette breaks. She was four or five years older than me, shorter, plumper, stronger. She spoke in pronouncements and I saw her future—Francis handing over his pay packet on Friday evenings, the two of them rearing decent reliable sons who'd work in the factories, marry young and start the same cycle all over again.

'Jesus, what are you? A nun or something?' scoffed Angela. Angela was blunt and a little frightening; she would call the men over when they passed at the end of lunch hour and tease them. But Marion was immune to Angela, to all of us. One day she said, 'If I as much as eat one Rich Tea finger I can feel it going straight to my hips.' I was lying on the grass watching a jet cross the sky. I thought of the journey of the little biscuit down the short lumpen body to her hips. She lived with her widowed mother and her older sick brother in a terraced house in Bohermore. She was the sole breadwinner. I had known girls like her in school—old beyond their years, tough, proud, cunning, who would hold things together for others, no matter what. She was the kind of girl who wore flesh-coloured tights and pencil skirts but never jeans, and would grow into the kind of woman I never wanted to be.

Gus lived about three miles from us at home but I had never once spoken to him. I used to see him in his car after Mass on Sundays, waiting for his mother, as my mother steered us kids to our car and my father stood in a huddle of men at the side door of the church. I saw him in the village, too, at the petrol pump or coming out of the shop with his messages. One evening in May my mother drove me up a dry rutted lane to his house to ask for the lift to the city.

'Tell him it'll only be for the summer, it's only a summer job,' she said as I got out.

'No, I better not,' I said. 'Come in with me.'

We walked up the path under trees, between two strips of overgrown garden. There was a line of smoke coming out the chimney. The two-storey house had once been handsome but the paintwork and masonry were flaking and crumbling and the wood at the base of the front door was rotten. At the side of the house there was a row of slate-roofed barns. An old bicycle lay under a tree and a wooden barrel stood at the gable end of the house to catch water from a downpipe. My mother rapped lightly on the door and then stepped well back. Inside on the windowsill I could see a pile of ancient looking paperbacks, their spines faded from the sun. I tilted my head to read the titles—*The Big Sky*, *The Virginian*, *Hopalong Cassidy*, *Riders of the Purple Sage*.

There was a shuffle and the door scraped open. He wore no shoes and his grey woollen jumper was stained. A black and white sheepdog sheltered timidly behind his legs. In the dark interior I saw the white banisters of the stairs. At the sight of us Gus's eyes grew panicked. He and my mother knew each other and after they had exchanged greetings, she told him what we wanted. I think that he'd have consented to almost anything just to close the door and be left in peace again.

We walked down the path and the sunlight fell through the trees onto my head. I thought of the lines of a poem I had learnt in school... Dapple-dawn-drawn Falcon. But I remembered it now as Dapple-dawn-drawn *light*, because the light flowing through the branches touched me and enveloped me in a new and strange way, as if I were encountering trees and leaves and light for the very first time. I thought of that poem and all the poems in my book, and felt the pull of all the books that would cross my path if I went to college that autumn. I felt a sudden calm, a sense of promise, and I'd like to have remained there for a little while under those trees.

'That's an awful way to live,' my mother said when we got into the car. 'The people who went before him would be ashamed.' She reversed the car and faced it onto the lane. 'D'you know we're distant relations?'

I turned to her. 'How distant?'

'Oh, second or third cousins—my mother and his mother were second cousins, I think.'

'Well, B-Baby Face, were they all nice to you in there today?' Gus asked me one Friday evening as we set off to pick up Martha. His arm was almost touching mine. I could smell the previous night's alcohol seeping from his pores. There were other smells too and I tried not to think of his body. When he spoke he hung his head a little and lowered his voice. I knew he was trying to deflect from his body and in the effort his words came out full of apology and shame.

He had dubbed me Baby Face from the start. Little by little we had grown accustomed to each other, and when we were alone he spoke in a slightly conspiratorial voice.

'They were,' I replied. 'They were grand.'

'I hope Marion is nice to you.'

'She is. She's very nice.'

And then my heart sank and I reddened. One day under the trees the factory girls had quizzed me about where I was from and what school I'd gone to and if I had a boyfriend. They were all from the city. Then Marion said. 'You get a lift with that Gus fella, don't you?'

'I do.'

'Jesus. You're some girl! And you don't mind sitting there beside him in the car?'

I shook my head and felt all their eyes on me.

'How d'you stick it—the BO? I'd say that fella never took a bath in his whole born life. Every single girl that ever came into the place here was afraid to go near him, d'you know that? He's like… something out of a zoo!'

She kept looking at me. 'They're a bit strange from your part of the country, aren't they?'

My heart took fright. 'I don't know. Are they?'

She tilted her head. 'Oh, you get pockets of it everywhere, indeed,' she said, and for a second she had a soft look and I thought I was safe. But then she said 'We had a guy here a few years ago. He was a porter up at the Visitors' Centre for a while. Came from your part of the country too—he knew Gus. They used to go up to Coen's at lunchtime every day and knock back a few. He got shown the door eventually because you couldn't have that kind of thing— the smell of drink—you couldn't have that kind of thing and the tourists walkin' in the door past him.' She turned to me again. 'Seanie Ryan… that was the porter. D'you know him?'

I shook my head. 'Don't know any Seanie Ryan.'

'Anyway, on our staff night out that Christmas he told me a story. He was well jarred but I believed him. He said when he was young he knew Gus's father, and that he was an alko too and spent his whole life drinking and fighting. I said to Seanie you'd never guess from Gus, would you!' The others laughed. I wanted to say that Gus doesn't fight.

'Anyway this guy Seanie tells me this story… he says that Gus's father himself used to tell it in the pub… It was a summer years ago and your man—Gus's father—was in the bog, cuttin' turf, and it was an awful hot day and of course your man got thirsty, and he set off across the bog in the direction of the nearest pub, two or three miles away. And when he got there he told the barman how a terrible thirst had come on him in the bog. "So I tied the young fella to the cart," he said, "and headed off walking…" And he did, too, Seanie said, he did, too! He tied the son to the cart and left him there all day in the sun. And that was Gus! Gus was the son!'

I had grown used to seeing him cross the factory floor, and come to know the intervals of his crossings. In the first weeks I timed my own little trips to the sink so that our paths might cross and I might hear a familiar voice from my own country. He never spoke, just nodded and turned his eyes down and continued on his way. There was something vague and distant about him inside the factory. Other men would pass with their trolleys or machinery and they'd wink and flirt and say 'How ya doin', sweetheart?' and make me blush. Gus would plough on, lugging his wagon past the sinks and the tables and the kilns, purple-faced and sweating, as if he'd drawn the clay up from the bowels of the earth.

When she finished her story Marion turned to me. 'He's an oddity all right… And you're a great girl to stick that car every day…' Then she peered at me. 'You're not related to him or anything, are you?'

'No! Jesus, no! No way! Are you mad!'

Angela, lying lazily against a tree, drew deeply on her cigarette and exhaled slowly. 'He's a fuckin' freak, that Gus, a fuckin' freak,' she said.

I watched his large hands and dirty nails on the steering wheel as we set off. His breathing was laboured and I thought any minute now his sweat will come seeping through the jacket and drown the two of us.

'D'you like the rhododendrons?' he asked.

I looked out the window as we rolled down the drive. 'Which ones are rhododendrons?'

'The pink ones, with the shiny leaves.'

'Yeah, they're nice.'

'They grow wild in some places, people think they're a scourge.' After a pause he took a deep breath, and exhaled. 'It's like an oven in there... So much for the earth, water, air and fire. There's not much air in there these days, that's for sure.'

I gave him a puzzled look. I never minded revealing my ignorance to Gus. His eyelashes were caked with clay and I wondered if, when he blinked, he heard the tiniest sound, like a butterfly might hear from its own flapping wings.

'*Fine bone china*,' he said, 'made with the four elements...' He looked at me again, and nodded out the window. 'That's what the brochures in there say. Earth, water, air and fire—that's what goes into the china. Who'd ever have thought it?' And then he looked out the window 'The same stuff we're all m-made of, or so they say... I read once that a man is really only a bag of water.'

'Will we stop for a mineral?' he asked after we passed Carnlough Cross. We were miles into the country now, Martha, Gus and I, our own little tribe, regrouped and reunited again.

Every Friday evening we stopped at the Half Way House, ten miles from home. I had not yet started to drink so Gus bought me a 7-Up. Martha got the second round. I did not know what to do, or how to be, or if, in the eyes of Gus and Martha, I had crossed far enough over the threshold into adulthood to buy a round of drinks.

'James and I are going to Dublin this weekend,' Martha

announced when we were all sitting around the little table in the empty bar.

Gus smiled and nodded at me. 'Oh, Baby Face, I hope you have a hat!'

I looked from Gus to Martha, lost again. Martha stiffened. 'We're going up on business actually. James has to go for work. We're making a weekend of it.'

Gus looked chastened.

'D'you go up there often?' I asked Martha.

'Now and again. We go to a hotel a few times a year.' And then she forgot herself. 'I love walking down Grafton Street on Saturday mornings with James. We got the ring in Appleby's—well, it's a good while ago now. They bring you into a private room at the back, and they have these lovely velvet tables and armchairs, and dishes with sweets and they serve champagne, and you can take your time choosing.' Her eyes shone in a way I had not seen before.

'It must be very nice,' I said, and then nearly gave myself away by saying I'd probably be going to Dublin to college myself soon. I had not told anyone in the china factory of my intentions. I had been taken on as a bona fide permanent employee. 'Do you go to Dublin much, Gus?' I asked.

'Ah, only a few times ever, Baby Face—I used to go to Croke Park to an odd hurling match when I was young. The last time I was up there was for a funeral... well, a sort of funeral. There was no coffin and no grave. A first cousin of mine who died in London, and they brought him home in a small pot. Me mother was alive at the time. There was just the Mass, and the pot of ashes was left above on a small table beside the altar.'

'I didn't think the Church allowed cremation back then,' Martha said.

'I don't know now... That was about fifteen years ago.'

We were quiet then. On the wall above the pool table the clock chimed six times. I thought of home and the evening ahead, my mother getting the tea, my father and brothers coming in after baling a field of hay, all of us around the table. I imagined Gus at his own table, bent over his books, straining to catch the last light of evening. I imagined empty bottles thrown out the back, stuffed into fertiliser bags and thrown under a tree. I saw him rising from the table and standing at the back door gazing out across fields or up at the sky.

'There's a lot to be said for that cremation business,' he said in a slow, thoughtful way. 'I don't know about being buried. I don't know if I'd like that. Unless maybe I could have three coffins, like the popes get. To keep the worms out!' and he turned to me and winked.

'I'd like to be buried up on the hill in Clonkeen,' Martha said. You're getting married, I wanted to tell her, not dying.

I proved to be a prize sponger. Annie, the supervisor, a neat middle-aged woman with glasses, called me Miss Feather Fingers. One afternoon in August she came whizzing towards me with word that I was to go to the Office. The next morning I was seated at a desk at the other end of the factory, with a turntable by my side, learning how to apply gold leaf to the rims of large china plates. The plates were glazed and decorated with blue cornflowers. My hands grew hot and pink and swollen from gripping the narrow brush. The art staff smiled and offered help, but I was confused and out of my depth. I missed the gossip and banter of the spongers and there was no radio to absorb my turbulent thoughts. I struggled with the turntable and with my conscience—I had a heavy heart—my guilt for having accepted this promotion and not revealing the truth about my future plans. I kept looking around me. I did not know how to stop things advancing.

I'd had no sightings of the spongers all morning. I longed for lunch hour when I would sit with them on the lawn and explain everything. I slipped into fantasies of long days in the future among library stacks and the sound of pages turning and my pen racing furiously across white paper. My heart pounded at the thought of it all and I knew then the arc my life would take.

'Where's Marion?' I asked when I joined the girls on the lawn.

No one answered and I felt their disdain. After a moment someone said she wasn't back from Mervue yet, that she'd gone to the post office. The others ignored me. I said I hated my new job, that the art girls were stuck-up and it was too quiet and boring as hell up there.

'Huh, the money won't bore you,' Angela said.

'No one said anything about money. I'm only on trial. I might not be kept at all.'

'Yeah, right!'

In the distance a loudspeaker cracked open the air. The voice crackled indistinctly—some local politician canvassing support, I thought—and it stopped and started and then moved off. I closed my eyes for a moment. I knew I would have to re-earn my place among the girls. An engine roared out on the road. I turned my head. A car with a trailer hitched to the back swung in the gate. It travelled up the drive and then revved and swerved and bumped over the stone kerb onto the grass. Someone said, Jesus, as it came to a stop in the centre of the lawn. The driver's door swung open and a man hopped out and began to throw lumps of iron from the trailer onto the grass. We stood and stepped forward into the sun.

'Jesus, that's Vinnie,' Angela said.

'Vinnie? Marion's brother? What's he doing here?' someone asked.

'Quick. Get Marion. Go on!'

'She's not back yet.'

A small crowd began to form. He was thin, with pale skin and jet black hair. He flung the iron heavily onto the grass. I squinted. They were iron sculptures, in human form. I saw a head, a hand, square shoulders, a sea of limbs landing on the grass. Their weight made gashes in the lawn. He stopped then and looked up. His eyes moved slowly along the line until they met mine. He looked directly at me, into me, and said something that I could not hear. Suddenly I felt doomed. I backed up a few steps to the low perimeter wall. He turned and walked to the car, opened the boot and lifted out a shotgun. Small cries went up, and I heard running feet around me. I bent low behind the wall, but my eyes remained rooted to him. He released the bolt and loaded the gun and fired three shots into the air. He circled the car and jumped on the bonnet and surveyed the whole place. He took a deep breath and opened his mouth. *'Let man and beast be covered with sackcloth, and cry mightily unto God, cry mightily unto God, for the Day of Judgement is at Hand...'* He spoke slowly. The porter ran along under the trees, bending low. *'I hear the sound of the Angel's trumpet...'* His volume increased. *'The angel of death will drag your souls from your mouths and will smite your faces... For the seventh seal has been opened by the Lamb of God... and the great harlot has been destroyed... and the beast has been set loose... and the oceans have turned to blood.'*

A shot rang out and then another, and he jumped to the ground and fired a volley into the sky. I covered my ears and sank lower. There was silence then. When I looked up he was walking over the windscreen and onto the roof of the car. His steps were delicate, graceful.

'And I saw a great white throne, and the earth and the heavens fled away. And I saw the dead, small and great, stand before God; and the books were opened and the dead were judged according to their works...'

His voice had begun to tremble and I thought: He will cry, and we will be saved. He leapt down and started to reload the gun.

And then I turned my head and saw Gus in his overalls come striding out of the factory yard, with his arms swinging by his side. He stepped onto the grass and crossed the lawn, and, as he drew near, the madman raised his head and smiled. *'Here come a man, here come a man,'* he called out, and he snapped closed the barrel of the gun and I felt the echo of its chamber inside my head. The madman's eyes opened wide, and then Gus put his hand on the madman's shoulder and drew his head close and said something, and then the two heads were bent and moving and talking. I thought an army of soldiers would leap over the wall in that second and wrestle the madman to the ground. But nothing stirred. Everything had ground to a halt. And then the two men turned and began to cross the lawn side by side, and they stepped over the kerb and onto the driveway and as they walked Gus put out his arm and the madman placed the gun in Gus's open hand. They walked to the entrance and passed through the gate and turned left up the Mervue Road and disappeared out of view.

I see news clips on TV sometimes of men going berserk in public places, men's minds going awry, and I think of how close it came that day. I don't know what Gus said to the madman. Ten minutes later he strolled back in the drive, walked up the granite steps of the Visitors' Centre, crossed the blue carpet and handed the gun in at Reception. Then he walked down the steps and around the back and for the rest of the afternoon he hauled his wagons back and forth across the factory floor until the hooter sounded at five o'clock.

I worked out the rest of the summer in the art department. Martha set her wedding date for July of the following year and I bought a round of drinks in the Half Way House on my last Friday of that summer. Marion stayed off work for two weeks and when she returned the girls closed ranks around her. I tried to imagine the two men strolling up the Mervue Road that day and Marion's incomprehension when she came upon them, and then the slow dawning reality at the sight of the gun, and the look that she and Gus must have exchanged as he handed Vinnie into her care.

Sometimes in the months following I'd be sitting in a packed lecture hall and I'd think of the spongers at their tables and the water turning white in their basins and every minute and hour unfolding, interminably, day after day. I'd think of my own family in the warm kitchen at night with the noise and the arguments and the TV blaring and Gus, alone with his Western novels, finding fidelity in far-off men, and I'd think of his hand reaching out and touching Vinnie's shoulder that day and the rarity of that, for Gus, the rarity of any human touch.

And then in my last year in college, during the coldest winter of my youth, my mother wrote me a rare letter. I sat at a table by an upstairs window in a redbrick house on Dublin's northside. I had spent the evening in the college library and my head was brimming with lines from John Donne's God sonnets. When I opened the envelope a fifty pound note fell from the pages of the letter. She wrote of the comings and goings on the farm, of my father and my younger siblings and their school work. And then:

I am sorry to tell you that your old friend Baby Face was found dead the other day. It was an awful sight, I believe, Lord have mercy on him. They think he went outside to get water from a barrel and he must have collapsed into the barrel somehow—he must have had a massive heart attack and fallen over, and that night was the start of this freezing cold weather we're having and didn't the water freeze solid, and that's the way the poor fellow was found. Everyone is talking about it. The funeral is tomorrow at eleven. Your father and I will go. He had no one left belonging to him. An awful ending entirely, the poor creature…

The sight of a bible in a hotel room now, or a drunk in a doorway, or my mother setting down her china cups, or even King Kong, all call Gus to mind. Or the word *meek*. Or a boy, any boy, any boy's eyes, evokes the small boy tethered in the sun and the thoughts that must have assailed him all day long. I remember Gus's aloofness inside the factory, and I know now that he was sparing me, that he understood how our association would contaminate me in the eyes of others. I remember the car journeys, the odours, and my own Judas moment. I think of him standing at his back door at night looking up at the drift of stars, pondering last things. I try to imagine what went through his mind when he staggered out to the barrel that cold night, or as he strode across the factory lawn that summer's day, bearing all of our realities in each stride. I think that something must have escaped and drained out of him into the other man that day. I wonder if he'd had an inkling that a gap would open and he would lever his way in between two orders, two domains, and when he reached out his hand and leaned his head towards Vinnie's, was it to the man or to the madness he spoke?

I think of our blood tie sometimes, mine and Gus's, and the ties that bind us all. I would have liked to have taken him with me that autumn, taken my own family too and the factory girls and made them all fit into my new world. I would have liked to have mitigated the loss and the guilt I felt at leaving them behind, the feeling that I was escaping and walking away. It is not an easy walk, I longed to tell them, but I'm not sure anyone was listening.

YOU FILL UP MY SENSES

She loves when she is alone with her mother in the car, like this. They are driving to check on the cattle and sheep in the summer grazing seven miles away. They stop at Burke's for petrol and buy loose pineapple cubes and cigarettes. Her mother smokes two cigarettes very quickly as if she'll be caught. Her mother never smokes in front of her grandmother. At night when her grandmother has gone to bed, and her mother and father and all the children are together in the kitchen—a normal family at last— she is happiest. Then her mother puts her youngest sister up to bed and afterwards walks along the landing calling out Holy Mary Mind Me so that her little sister will hear her voice and not be afraid, and her sister calls back Holy Mary Mind Me too, and they keep up this singsong as her mother comes down the stairs and in along the hall. Then her mother is in the kitchen making the supper. She is humming softly. The television is on. She watches her mother putting out the bowls and spoons, the sugar bowl and the milk jug. She loves her mother very much. When she grows up she wants to be exactly like her.

They walk to opposite ends of the land—her mother to count the cattle and she the sheep. She is nine now. As she tramples through the fields she forgets all about the sheep. She stands under a tree looking up at the undersides of the leaves and the little veins almost make her weak. She walks on, avoiding the thistles and the cow dung until she gets to the hill. There are crooked stones on the far side where unbaptised babies were buried long ago. She stands at the top of the hill. She opens her arms wide and runs down the hill, her hair blowing, her eyes watering in the breeze. She goes up the hill again and stands still and starts to sing. She raises her face to the sun. She would like to be a singer on TV. She would like to make her mother and father proud. She would like to bring tears to their eyes.

Her mother is not cross when she finds her—her mother is never cross with her. Together they start to count the sheep. How many are in the other field, her mother asks her, and she runs to the gap and counts them and runs back again, breathless, and the number is right. They walk back to the car. She hands her mother a pineapple cube from the paper bag and as they drive home they make sucking noises and laugh. Her mother is not like other mothers. She is young and girlish and runs in the mothers' race on sports days and tickles her and her brothers and sisters at bedtime and grinds sweets as hard and fast as they do. On Sundays when they have Neapolitan ice cream for dessert, her mother takes spoonfuls from her own bowl and drops them into the bowls of her younger brother and sister until her own ice cream is almost gone. She does not know how her mother can bear to give away her ice cream. She does not mind not getting any from her mother's bowl, and her mother knows this. Her mother understands everything about her.

As they drive her mother sighs. When her mother is far away like this she tries to bring her back. She asks her about her life when she was a child. Were there really three hundred and sixty-five windows in your house? she asks, though she already knows the answer.

—Yes, one for every day of the year, her mother says.

—And two stairs?

—Two stairs. One lovely wide one in the front hall and a narrow one near the back kitchen.

Her mother's home was called Easterfield. She remembers it from when she was very small, a big house with tall windows and a wide lawn facing the wrong way—facing out to the fields instead of to the road—and a gravel yard with barns where her father parked the car. And upstairs long landings with creaking floorboards and rooms with no light bulbs, and the creepy backstairs at the far end. She has a faint memory of her mother's father with snow-white hair and round glasses sitting by the range holding a red plastic back scratcher in his hand. The house is all closed up now. On the day of her mother's fourth birthday a blackbird flew into the dining room and tore a piece of wallpaper from a spot above the window. The wallpaper had swirling ivy and serpents, and was very old. She sees her four-year-old mother standing in the room looking up at the blackbird. Suddenly her thoughts turn dark. She is getting too close to the sadness of her mother's life.

At home her father and her older brother are gathering in the sheep and lambs and flocking them in the yard, for dosing. She hates when there are big jobs going on. The night before the sheep-shearing or silage-making or cattle-testing she cannot sleep. She lies there, rehearsing it all in her mind, searching for dangers—open gates, charging cattle, escaping children—or the rage of her father when an animal breaks loose or the baler breaks down. By morning she is exhausted, and all day long she keeps watch. She is not as quick at the farm work as her brother and sister—at turning the turf or stacking the bales—and she is relieved when evening comes. She is always waiting for evenings and happy endings.

In the yard her father and her brother make hooshing sounds at the sheep and Captain the sheepdog rushes in and nips them on the legs. When they are penned tightly she looks in through the rungs of the gate at the ewes' big faces. They look calmly back at her. She has the feeling that they know more than she does and

23

that, somehow, like her mother, they understand her. And maybe even love her.

One day when she was seven she turned to her mother, smiling, and said, What was your mammy like? Her mother stopped for a second.

—I never knew my mother, she said. She died when I was three. A week later the bird flew in and tore the wallpaper in the dining room.

The mother was in bed, coughing, for a long time and her mother's older sisters came home from boarding school to mind her and their baby brother. Her mother remembers being lifted up on the bed to give her mother a kiss.

—She had a white nightdress on and long hair. I put out my hand to touch her hair but they must have thought I was going to pull it so they lifted me down and took me away.

She wanted to say something but she was afraid she would make her mother cry.

—She told my sisters which dress to lay her out in. And to be sure to use the linen tablecloth for the meal after the funeral. I remember the men carrying the coffin down the stairs.

Her mother stands on the steps at the front door and calls her in. In the kitchen her grandmother is sitting by the range knitting. She tells her to take the brush and sweep the floor. Afterwards she plays with her small sister and brother on the floor. Her other sister, who is eight and the middle child, is cutting out cardboard shapes with scissors that are too big for her hands. Her mother is making bread at the kitchen table, and every now and then turns to check the steaming saucepans on the cooker. Her mother is always working, inside and out—putting down fires, making meals, bringing in turf. She is always tired. Sometimes at Mass she falls asleep and she or her sister has to wake her up to stand for the prayers. The work is never done. Every week brings new jobs on the farm. She tries to see ahead and help her mother—she hoovers the house on Sunday mornings before Mass and stuffs the chicken and sews up its behind with a needle and thread, the way her grandmother taught her.

It is not her father's fault, all this work—he is tired too. But at night when he sits down to watch television, her mother is still at the cooker frying the tea, or at the table making apple tarts, or ironing, and the television is blaring and the kitchen is hot and the younger kids are arguing and fighting. Sometimes her mother snaps at her father and her father snaps back and her grandmother tells the kids crossly to have manners and then her mother cries. One winter's night her mother flung a plate of rashers and sausages down on the table in front of her father and ran out of the kitchen. The food bounced on the plate. She followed her mother into the hall, begging her, but her mother put on her purple coat and walked out the front door. She ran after her, pulling at the coat, crying Come back, but her mother ran down the steps, and off into the night. She stood at the open door not knowing which way to turn. She thought she should be loyal to her mother but the little ones were crying in the kitchen. She ran in to her father. She's gone, she cried. Are you happy now? His face was dark and lonely. She remembered that look on him before, when she woke one night and came down for a drink, and he was sitting in the armchair watching a film. Go after her, she said softly, you have to go after her. But he just sat there, sad and silent. When the kids were fed she stood at the front door again looking out into the dark. Her heart was shattered. Then her grandmother called her in. An hour later she heard the front door close quietly and her mother's footsteps on the stairs. Later when she went up to her own room her mother was in her bed. She put her arms around her and kissed the top of her head. Her mother only ever kisses her when she is sad. She thought her mother must have walked to the end of the lane, and might have kept going if the lane hadn't ended.

*

The dinner is ready and she goes outside and calls down to her father and brother in the yard. Her brother is inside the pen, holding a lamb like a baby in his arms, its legs in the air. She knows that sometimes they are happy, the whole family is happy. Some mornings when they are at the breakfast and her mother is standing by her father's side pouring out his tea he touches her waist and she sees the look they give each other. Last winter when her grandmother went on holidays to an uncle's house, her father carried the record player out to the kitchen every night and put on Jim Reeves, and taught herself and her sister to dance. He lifted them, in turn, onto his stockinged feet and waltzed them around the floor. When they were finished she said to him, Dance with Mammy, and she ran and tugged on her mother's arm. But her mother was tired. She was sewing buttons on a jacket. Her father stayed standing in the middle of the kitchen for a minute with his arms by his side, staring at the tiles.

At the dinner table an argument starts and her middle sister grabs a crayon from her small brother's hand and he starts to bawl. Give it back to him, her mother tells her. It's mine, her sister says. She doesn't care. She gives backchat to her mother and father all the time. To her grandmother too. Her mother is cutting open an apple tart now. Sometimes she is helpless; she does not know what to do or how to be a mother. She gives her sister a look across the table but her sister is defiant. The little brother thumps her sister and she thumps him back, harder, and her father shouts at her. Her grandmother says, That's the family ye're rearing now. Her sister looks across at her grandmother. Shut up, you, she says. Her heart is pounding and she kicks her sister under the table to make her stop. But her sister keeps on going. Then as her grandmother turns to get up from the table her mother reaches across and slaps her sister on the elbow with the tip of the bread knife. Her sister's

26

mouth falls open and she howls. Blood falls from her elbow onto her plate. Her mother has a terrified look and she jumps up and runs to the sink. Her father's face darkens and his mouth clenches in anger. She expects he will pound the table with his fist and knock over the chair and storm out. But he doesn't move. He is staring at her mother. They are all staring at her mother, and at the big drops of blood falling on the plate. She doesn't feel sorry for her sister at all—her heart is raging at her sister.

After the dinner her father and brother go back out to the sheep and she walks around the back of the house. There are a few puffy clouds at the far end of the sky. The afternoon is very still, and the day seems long. She goes back inside, to the sitting room and sits at the piano. The room is full of sunlight. She practises her scales three times, and the arpeggios three times, and then the piece from her exam book three times, too. When she is finished she opens the sideboard and takes out the wedding album. Her father and mother are about to walk down the aisle. She knows their whole story— how they met, their wedding, their honeymoon. She has asked her mother many times. She has read, too, the little piece clipped from the local newspaper. Her mother's dress was embroidered French brocade, ballet length. She carried a bouquet of pink carnations and maidenhead fern. There were seventy guests at the wedding breakfast. The happy couple toured the south of Ireland on their honeymoon.

She turns the pages slowly, searching their faces. Their shyness almost makes her cry. And knowing that their wedding day is over, over and gone forever, and they will never be this happy again. There is a photograph taken on the honeymoon at the back of the album. They are standing at the bonnet of a black car, smiling. The lakes of Killarney are behind them. Her mother is wearing a white sleeveless blouse and her Dorene skirt, the pale grey wool skirt that hangs under plastic in her wardrobe. It is the most beautiful skirt, with green and pink lines, the same bright pink as a stick of rock. Sometimes when they are going on a day out to the seaside she runs into her mother's room and tells her to put it on. She thinks if her mother wears the Dorene skirt she might forget all about the work and the arguments and the five kids, and she and her father might be in love again, and happy. She gazes at their faces in the honeymoon photograph. They do not know what is ahead of them. If they knew what was ahead of them they might never have left the lakes of Killarney.

She hears her father's voice and looks out the window. A lamb has escaped through the gate and her brother runs after it and scoops it up. She puts the wedding album away and goes to the record player and puts on a John Denver record. His photograph is on the cover. She sits back on the couch and he starts to sing. Rocky Mountain High. Sunshine on my Shoulders. She thinks of her father out in the fields all summer long. Sounds from the kitchen drift down the hall: the clatter of delft, the radio, her mother's voice. She gets up and sits at the piano and places her fingers on the keys. She hears the back door close, and footsteps coming around the gable end. She plays high C. Her mother is crossing the yard. She plays each note, C, B, A, C, B, A and hums. She feels the sun on her mother's face. She closes her eyes. *You fill up my senses.*

In the late afternoon her mother drives her and her sister to town for their weekly music lesson. Did ye practise yere piano pieces? her mother asks. Yes, Mammy, she says. Her sister has her knees up on the back of the seat and hardly answers.

She goes in first for her music lesson, and her mother and sister walk down the street to the supermarket. Mrs Walsh, her teacher, is strict but every week she praises her. Good girl, she says when she plays her scales. Mr Walsh enters and sets down a tray with a cup and saucer, a tiny jug of milk, a plate with French toast and a pot of tea, kept warm under a tea cosy. It smells delicious and the crunch of the French toast makes her mouth water. The room is very warm. Mrs Walsh is sitting so close to her she can hear her swallowing. She follows the sound of the tea and toast travelling down into Mrs Walsh's stomach and the click of the knife and fork on the plate and the cup touching down on the saucer, and when she starts playing her exam piece she cannot bring her mind back, and her fingers trip each other and she makes mistakes on nearly every line.

Then it is her sister's turn. She and her mother sit under a tree in the church grounds, and wait. Her mother takes off her sandals. The air is heavy and silent, as if there is something between them, waiting to be said. Her mouth goes dry. Suddenly she knows what it is. She has been waiting for it for weeks. Her mother is sick. One morning a month ago, she woke up early and walked along the landing to the bathroom, very sleepy. Her mother was walking ahead of her and did not hear her coming behind. Her mother's feet were bare. Her nightdress came to her knees. And then she saw the blood, bright and fresh, at the back of her mother's nightdress. She froze. Her mother kept on going and turned into the bathroom.

An old lady walks by and smiles at them and enters the church. Her mother is leaning against the tree. She watches her closely, afraid that any minute now she will clear her throat and start to speak the dreadful news. But her mother just tilts her head back and closes her eyes. She wonders if cancer makes you tired. That day of the bleeding her mother was pale and quiet. She watched her all the time; she followed her around the kitchen and outside for turf. That night she could not sleep. She lay listening to the sounds of the house and praying for her mother and waiting for morning to come. In the dark she remembered all the things her mother had ever told her. She imagined the small girl her mother was, and the dining-room table set for the funeral meal and the bird flying out the window with the ivy in its beak. She doesn't know how anyone could eat a meal after burying a mother.

Her sister crosses the street after her music lesson. Her mother has dropped off to sleep against the tree. If her mother has cancer and if she dies, then they will be the same—they will both have had a dead mother. She and her sister rouse her mother now. She hops up quickly, her eyes bright, and she looks strong again. Her legs are strong. Her voice is strong. On the way back to the car they buy three Super Split ice creams and on the drive home they are quiet and content, concentrating on the ice creams. She tries to make hers last, but she keeps looking over at her mother and she licks too hard and too fast. Her mother is talking about what has to be done when they get home. She thinks the danger has passed and that her mother might be okay after all. If her mother is okay she will thank God for the rest of her life.

Late in the evening she finds her brother sitting on the wall of the pen. Captain is lying at the edge of the yard, his head resting on his paws, his eyes following her. She can hear the engine of a tractor out on the main road. The day's work is done, and her sisters and small brother are inside, playing, and her father is drifting around the farm—closing gates, tidying the shed, folding old fertiliser bags.

—What happened? she asks her brother. The pen is filthy and wet from the sheep dirt, but it is not that. Where did all the blood come from? she asks. What were ye doing?

—Squeezing the lambs, he says.

—What's that? she asks, pointing to the corner. There is a heap of blood and guts in the dirt, and little circles of grey wool. They are like woollen hats for tiny dolls.

—That's where he cut them underneath with the penknife. He cut them and squeezed out the little yokes. He had to pull out the guts with the pinchers.

She cannot look at him. One day he hurt himself on the bar of his bicycle on the way home from school. Did you hurt yourself underneath? her grandmother asked him when they got home. He couldn't talk with the pain. She remembers when her mother used to bath herself and her brother together on Saturday nights. She knows that the underneath in boys is soft and easily hurt.

She is scraping the sole of her sandal on the edge of a brick. She is afraid to look, but still she turns her head a little towards the corner. The flies are swarming around. The guts are like short fat worms, creamy-pink and shiny, with little veins all over them. There are dozens of small pale balls, like raw meat, among them. And the little wool caps. She presses her hand on her belly button and for a second she cannot breathe.

—They have to be castrated, her brother says, so they won't grow into rams.

She is running down the road to the Well Field, Captain running beside her. She stands outside, looking through the rungs of the gate. They are all lying down over by the ditch, the lambs pressed against their mothers' bodies. She is thinking of their underneaths, open and sore, against the ground. As she watches a lamb rises slowly. The mother rises too and the lamb lowers his head under her, for milk. He pauses and stands there. Then his front legs fold at the knees and he is down again. The mother kneels too and the lamb lets out a thin feeble bleat. She has never heard such a sound.

She finds her mother at the clothesline at the back of the house. The pine trees are leaning over them, making everything darker. As soon as she starts telling her mother, the tears come.

—They have to do it, her mother says. It's the way things are done. She is taking clothes off the line, shirts, pants, towels, and folding them into the laundry basket.

—They weren't dosing them at all this morning, she sobs. You said they were dosing.

Her mother says nothing. She takes the clothes pegs off her father's socks.

—Don't be thinking about it, she says then. Put it out of your mind.

—They shouldn't have cut them like that.

Her mother moves along the line, drags a sheet off roughly, folds it from the corners.

—They're not able to stand up, she says.

—They don't feel anything, they're only animals. Her mother is frowning. She kicks the laundry basket to move it along.

—They're bleeding, she cries. Below in the field now, they're bleeding.

—God Almighty, will you ever stop! Will you? Will you ever just leave me alone?

The sun is setting. The little birds are sleeping in the trees. She stands at the gable end of the house, her head tilted, listening. Now and then she hears a single bleat in the distance. Soon it will be dark and everything will be silent. They will lie huddled against their mothers, all night long. She goes inside. They are all there, in the kitchen. The nine o'clock news is on. There's a big search for a little girl who has gone missing on a bog. There are men out looking for her, beating down the heather with sticks.

She is afraid her heart is turning. And that her mother will know this, and then her mother's heart will turn too. She thinks there is no one in the whole world as lonely as her mother.

THINGS I SEE

Outside my room the wind whistles. It blows down behind our row of houses, past all the bedroom windows and when I try to imagine the other bedrooms and the other husbands and wives inside, I hear my own husband moving about downstairs. He will have finished reading the paper by now and broken up the chunks of coal in the grate. Then he will carry the tray into the kitchen, carefully, with the newspaper folded under his arm. He will wash the mugs and leave them to drain; he will flip up the blind so that the kitchen will be bright in the morning. Finally, he will flick off the socket switches and pick up his bundle of keys. Occasionally, just, he pauses and makes himself a pot of tea to have at the kitchen table, the house silent around him. I know the way he sits, his long legs off to the side, the paper propped against the teapot, or staring into the corner near the back door, pensive. He drinks his tea in large mouthfuls and gives the mug a discreet little lick, a flick of the tongue, to prevent a drip. When I hear his chair scrape the tiles I switch off my lamp and turn over. Don is predictable and safe. Tonight he is making himself that last pot of tea.

There are nights when I want to go down and shadow him and stand behind his chair and touch his shoulder. My pale arms would encircle his neck and I would lean down so that our faces touch. Some nights between waking and sleeping I imagine that I do this but I stand and watch him from the kitchen door and I am aware only of the cold tiles under my bare feet. There is something severe and imperious in Don's bearing that makes me resist. He has a straight back and square shoulders and black black hair. His skin is smooth and clear, without blemish, as if he has many layers of perfect epidermii. Beside him, with my pale skin and fair hair, I am like an insignificant underground animal, looking out at him through weak eyes.

Lucy, my sister, is staying with us for a week. She is sleeping in the next room and when she tosses I hear the headboard knock against the wall. I get up and stand at the window. The light from the kitchen illuminates the back garden and the gravel path down to the shed. When I am away from this house I have to let my mind spill over into this room before I can sleep. I have to reconstruct it in the strange darkness of another room before I can surrender. Its window bears on the old fir trees looming tall and dark beyond the back wall. There is the house and these trees and a patch of sky above and these are my borders. They pen me in and I like this. I cannot bear large vistas, long perspectives, lengthy hopes. When we first came here Don wanted us to take the front room; it is west-facing and sunny and looks onto the street. He likes to hear the sounds of the neighbourhood; he likes to know there are lives going on around us. Some nights he sleeps out there. This evening he told me I was intolerant.

Tonight I long to be alone. I would walk around the carpeted rooms upstairs, straightening curtains, folding clothes, arranging things. I would lie on the bed and inhale Don's scent on the pillow and this contact, this proximity to him, would be enough to make me nervous and excitable, too hopeful. Sometimes when Don and Robin are out and I am alone in the house I am prone to elation, swept up in some vague contentment at the near memory of them.

I let myself linger in their afterglow, and then something—a knock on the door, a news item on the TV, the gas boiler firing up outside—will shatter it all. Lately I have become concerned for our future. It is not the fact of growing old, but of growing different. Don gets impatient if I say these things and I see his face change and I know he is thinking, For God's sake, woman, pull yourself together.

I go into the bathroom and the light stings my eyes. I splash water on my face. He will hear my movements now. I rub on cream and massage the skin around my eyes and cheek bones. My eyes are blue, like Lucy's. There are four girls in my family and we all have blue eyes. I go out on the landing and lean over the banisters and check the line of light under the kitchen door. I pause outside Lucy's door. I imagine her under the bedclothes, the sheet draped over her shoulders, her hair spilling onto the pillow. Lucy is a musician; she plays the cello in an orchestra and this evening she played a Romanian folk dance in our living room. Robin was in her jammies, ready for bed and afterwards she picked up Lucy's bow. Lucy let her turn it over carefully and explained about horsehair and rosin and how string instruments make music and she showed her how to pluck a string. Then she whisked her up into her arms and nuzzled her and breathed in my daughter's apple-scented hair.

'Have you thought about music lessons for her?' she asked me a moment later. 'She could learn piano, or violin. She's old enough, you know.' Before I could reply she brought her face close to Robin's. 'Would you like that, Sweetheart—would you like to play some real *mu-sic*?' Robin giggled and clung to Lucy like a little monkey. They sat on the sofa across from me. A bluebottle came from nowhere and buzzed above my head.

'I don't know,' I said. 'She's already got so much going on. And she's only six.' I watched the bluebottle zigzag drunkenly towards the uplighter and for a second I was charged with worry. Every day insects fly into that lighted corner and land on the halogen bulb and extinguish themselves in a breath.

'Don't leave it too late, Annie. She's got an ear, she's definitely got an ear. I said so to Don today.'

She carried Robin upstairs then and they left a little scent in their wake. It reminded me of the cream roses that clung to the arched trellis in our garden at home. No, it reminded me of Lucy. I think she has always given off this scent, like she's discarding a surfeit of love. I wonder if all that wood and rosin and sheep gut suffocates her scent. I think of her sitting among the other cellists, her bulky instrument between her knees, her hair falling on one side of her face, the bow in her right hand drawing out each long mournful note, the fingers of her left hand pressed on the neck of the instrument or sliding down the fingerboard until I think she will bleed out onto the strings. I watched those hands today as they passed Robin a vase of flowers. She has taught Robin to carry the flowers from room to room as we move.

I turn and tiptoe into Robin's room. The lamplight casts a glow on her skin and her breathing is so silent that for a second I am worried and think to hold a tiny mirror to her mouth, the way nurses check the breath of the dying. She is a beautiful child, still and contained and perfect, and so apart from me that sometimes I think she is not mine, no part of me claims her. Don has stayed home and is raising her and she is growing confident. Often at work I pause midway through typing a sentence, suddenly reminded of them, and I imagine them at some part of their day: Don making her lunch, talking to her teacher, clutching her schoolbag and waiting up for her along the footpath. I have an endless set of images I can call on. This evening as I pulled into the drive Don was putting his key in the door. The three of them, Don, Lucy and Robin, had been for a walk. It was windy, they had scarves and gloves on and their cheeks were flushed. Lucy and

Robin laughed and waved at me as I pulled in. I sat looking at them all for a moment. Now I have a new image to call on.

If I ever have another child I will claim it—I will look up at Don after the birth and say 'This one's mine.' I have it all planned.

After dinner this evening Don took the cold-water tap off the kitchen sink. He spread newspapers and tools over the floor and cleared the cupboard shelves and stretched in to work on the pipes. He opened the back door and went out and back to the shed several times and cold air blew through the house. After a while there was a gurgle, a gasp, and a rush of water spilled out along the shelf onto the floor. He jumped back and swore. Robin was in the living room watching Nickelodeon and Lucy was practising in the dining room. I had been roaming about the house tidying up, closing curtains, browsing. I had stepped over Don a few times and over the toolbox and spanners and boxes of detergent strewn around him.

'What's up?' I asked finally. His head was in the cupboard. 'What are you at?' I pressed.

'Freeing it up,' he said, and I thought of the journey these three words had to make, bouncing off the base of the sink before ricocheting back out to me. 'Did you not notice how slow it's been lately?'

I leaned against the counter. The cello drifted in from the next room, three or four low-pitched notes, a pause, then the same notes repeated again.

'Wouldn't the plunger have cleared it?' I watched his long strong torso and his shoulders pressed against the bottom shelf. He drew up one leg as he strained to turn a bolt. His brown corduroys were threadbare at the right knee and the sight of this and the thought of his skin underneath made me almost forgive him. The cello paused and then started again and I focused on the notes, and tried to recognise the melody. Lucy favours Schubert; she tells me he is all purity. I have no ear and can scarcely recognise Bach.

'Is that urgent?' I asked.

'Nope.'

'Can't it wait then?'

I imagined his slow blink. Next door Lucy turned a page. I sensed her pause and steady herself before raising her bow again. A single sombre note began to unfurl into the surrounding silence and when I thought it could go on no longer and she really would bleed out of her beautiful hands, it touched the next note and ascended and then descended the octave and I thought this *is* Bach, this is that sublime suite that we listened to over and over in the early months of the pregnancy, and then never again, because Don worried that such melancholy would affect his unborn child.

'Can't you do these jobs during the day, when there's no one here?' I blurted. A new bar had begun and the music began to climb, to envelop, again.

He reversed out of the cupboard and threw the spanner in the box. 'What the hell is needling you this evening?'

'Shh. Keep your voice down. Please.'

It was Bach, and I strove to catch each note and draw out the title while I still could, before it closed in.

He began to gather up the tools and throw them in the toolbox. 'Jesus, we have to live.' I stood there half-listening. The music began to fade until only the last merciful note lingered. I can recognise the signs, the narrowing of his eyes as he speaks, the sourness of his mouth when he's hurt and abhorred and can no longer stand me, and when the music stopped I longed to stop too, and gaze at him until something flickered within and his eyes met mine and we found each other again.

He leaned towards me then and spoke in a low tight voice. 'What's wrong with you, Ann? Why're you so fucking intolerant?'

He slumped against the sink and stared hard at me and I looked out at the darkness beyond the window. I heard Lucy's attempt to muffle our anger with the shuffle of her sheet music and cello and stand. I longed for her to start up again, send out a body of sound that would enrapture, and then I wondered if he had heard it, if it had reached him under the sink all this time, and if he'd remembered or recognised or recalled it. *What was that piece*, I longed to ask him, *that sonata that Lucy played just now, the one we once loved, you and I?*

I thought of them, Lucy, Don and Robin at the front door earlier. They had all been laughing. Who had said something funny? Robin is sallow like her father, with long dark hair, and some strands had blown loose from her scarf. Don was laughing too but when he saw my car he averted his eyes and singled out the key in his bundle. There was a look on his face. I have seen that look before. It is a dark downcast look and when he looked away this evening perhaps he was remembering another day, the day that I was remembering too.

Robin was newly born and Lucy, having just finished college, came to stay for a few weeks, to relieve us at times with Robin. I had wanted a child for a long time and now, when I recall them, I think those early days were lived in a strange surreal haze. At night, sleepless, I would turn and look at Don in the warmth of the lamplight, his dark features made patient and silent by sleep, and I would want to preserve us—Don, Robin and me—forever in the present then, in that beautiful amber glow.

I had gone into the city that day and wandered about the parks and the streets, watching my happy face slide from window to window. Light-headed, euphoric, I bought cigarettes and sat outside a café and watched people's faces and felt a surge of hope. An old couple came out with a tray and sat down, hardly speaking but content. Young girls crowded around tables, flicking their long hair and chatting to boys. I lit a cigarette and bit off half of the chocolate that came with my coffee, saving the rest for later, to disguise the cigarette smoke on my breath. I had not smoked for years and the deep draw spiked my lungs and the surge of nicotine quickened my heartbeat and made my fingers tremble and I closed my eyes and relished the pure intoxication of it all.

Suddenly I was startled by a pigeon brushing my arm and landing at my feet. It fluttered and hopped on one leg and then I saw the damaged foot. There remained only one misshapen toe and its nail, ingrown, coiled tightly around the leg, swollen, sore, unusable. I met the pigeon's round, black empty eye and thought of the word *derelict* and it seemed like the saddest word I had ever encountered. Two more pigeons landed close by and pecked at crumbs. And then a gust of wind—tight against the street—blew in and tossed napkins and paper cups and wrappers from the tables. My chocolate, half-eaten in its gold-foil wrapper, blew to the ground. My pigeon hopped over and pecked at it and I smiled at his good fortune and then, in panic, thought that Don would now smell the cigarette when I got home. I checked my watch and remembered Robin and her tiny clenched fists and her moist eyelids, and wondered why I had ever left her. I went to rise and a terrible racket of flapping wings and screeching started up at my feet. The others had come after the chocolate. They had cornered my lame pigeon. 'Shoo, Shoo,' I called at them. I waved my arms and tried to rise again but with my shaking hands and my clamorous heart and the terrible screeching of pigeons, I fell back into the chair.

Later I fled the city, trembling, and drove fast towards the suburbs, with Robin on my mind and a sinking feeling that I might not see her again.

At the front door I reached into my pocket but found no key. I looked in the living-room window. Robin was asleep in her Moses basket. She was there, safe, and she was mine.

I walked around to the back of the house. The old fir trees were pressed flat against the sky and everything was still. The neighbourhood was silent and the birds and the dogs and the children's street play were all absent, or that is how I remember it, as if all living creatures had sensed danger and fled, as they do on high Himalayan or Alpine ground before an avalanche. The back door is half glass and Don had his back to me. I raised my hand to knock on the glass and then I saw Lucy, in front of him, wedged up against the counter. He stood over her, leaning into her, with an arm on each side of her and his palms flat on the counter. He was spread-eagled; he had her cornered. Her body and face were hidden from me; her hands moved on his shoulders, and then her fingers touched his neck, and her legs in jeans emerged from between his. I looked at the back of his head, at his thick black hair, his square shoulders. He was wearing a check shirt I had given him at Christmas, and his dark brown corduroy trousers. He moved his hips and his thighs, grinding her, and I thought: she is too small for him, he will crush her. But I underestimate Lucy.

And then he stopped moving and tilted his head, as if hearing something. He turned his face to the right and I slid back. All he would have caught was a shadow, like a bird's, crossing the back door. I walked lightly around to the front and sat in the car. Later I rang the doorbell and pretended to search for something in the boot. And things started to come out and move again. A jeep drove into the cul-de-sac and a child yelped and cycled his tricycle along the footpath. An alarm went off at the other end of the street. Finally Don opened the door.

'I forgot my keys,' I explained quickly. He looked at me, that too calm look.

'You should have come around the back. Robin might have woken with the bell.'

'Did she sleep the whole time?' I asked, and we looked at each other for a terrible moment and neither one of us heard his reply.

*

Now I hear his movements below and I become anxious. He is locking the back door. I have a sense of being in both places now—there, below with him, and here in the bed. My heart is thumping and I am far from sleep.

And then suddenly I am exhausted from the effort of tracking him. My bed is too warm, too familiar, like a sickbed. I am agitated, and I twist and turn and lie horizontally and try to use up all the space and I remember a childhood illness, a fever, and my mother's voice in the darkened room, saving me. And now I want Don here, I want the memory of him here. I want him beside me so that I can find the slope of his body and lie against it. I want him to reach across the wide bed and draw me into his arms. I want him to lay his large hand flat on my belly and press gently and feel desire flood through me. I want to be silent and dreamy and view this room, this sky, everything, from a different angle. I want to be shielded by trees and lie against him and sleep.

'You asleep?'

I did not hear him come upstairs. He has stolen upon me before I am prepared. He approaches my side of the bed but stands back a little. His voice is soft and defeated. I open my eyes and look at him. I am waiting for some sound to rise out from inside me, a few words to send across this short distance that will not disappoint. He waits too and a long look passes between us and I know something has spoilt, and then he moves away and starts to undress. And for the first time his undressing, piece by piece, is too intimate and crushing and revealing and I close my eyes and weep.

He goes into the bathroom and closes the door. In a moment I hear the flush and the brushing of teeth. When he returns he walks around the room and hangs up his clothes, unplugs the hairdryer, tidies away his shoes. Now and then he clears his throat in a precise, emphatic way. He does this when we argue—he appears occupied in his task, untouched, untroubled, aloof. He does it to distance me, to reduce me, to make me think, *This is nothing*. And I am left wondering—do I magnify everything, do I magnify the words and the pain and the silences? Do I?

He reaches for a pillow and for a moment I think he is going to take it to the front room. But he gets in beside me. He sits with his arms folded, looking from him, and I can feel the rise and fall of his chest. I wonder at his thoughts, at those clear thoughts I imbue him with, at his certainty, at how he seeks always to unscramble things when all I can summon is silence, and how I will never know him but always imagine him. Outside there is the occasional flapping of our clothes on the clothesline, and then the faint distant whistle of the wind, as if it has moved off and left our house alone tonight. And I think this is how things are, and this is how they will remain, and with every new night and every new wind I know that I am cornered too, and I will remain, because I cannot unlove him.

THE PATIO MAN

The house is quiet. He knows from the light in the room that it has rained. He rolls onto his stomach. In the flat above someone crosses the floor, uses the bathroom and returns, and the house falls silent again. A car drives by, and the rubbery sound of the tyres lingers on the wet street. He switches on the radio and listens to the forecast. He thinks of how clouds darken the mountain at home, and rain beats down on the faces of anyone walking on the shore. He falls back to sleep again. He dreams of a bear in his mother's garden, rooting for something, and then sloping off, large and lonesome in the distance.

Later he goes out to buy bread. The sun on the wet street dazzles him. Outside the big stone church he peels off his sweatshirt. Two girls climb out of a basement and walk ahead of him, pulling suitcases behind them. He wishes he had gone west for the weekend. Saturday night in Dublin leaves an ache in him. The parish football team is playing a semifinal on Sunday. The pub will be lively with locals and tourists and a few older emigrants home on holidays. He turns onto the main road and buys bread and a newspaper in the corner shop. A bus draws up outside. Sometimes in winter he goes to town, sits in a café and reads his paper, then browses the bookshops. He goes straight to the gardening sections and thumbs through the design books and memorises the plans.

He has grown to like the city a little in winter; there is more honesty, less artifice, people wear raincoats and strong shoes and keep their heads down.

Back in the flat he gets a text from Tom Burke to say he's going down home in the evening and if he likes, they can travel together. He pictures himself deep in Tom's passenger seat, the sun in his eyes, Tom doing most of the talking. He'll have the radio tuned to some soft rock station until they're out of Dublin. Then he'll switch over to RTÉ for the sports news. Tom will advise him to buy a house, while prices are low. Then they'll grow quiet and he'll slip into the soft hopeful phase of the journey. There will still be light when they arrive. He will sit with his mother and eat the meal she'll have cooked. He'll walk down to the shore, counting the sheep and cattle on the way, and at ten o'clock he'll head over to the pub. By eleven the younger ones will have left for Westport. The old men will drift off before twelve and he'll glance around, not wanting to be the last to leave. There is something empty in the walk home.

He drives his van south along familiar streets to the suburbs. He rolls down the window, glances at gardens and at the blank faces of other drivers, feels the breeze on his arm. Suburban gardens are overstocked, he thinks. Country people are more sparing in their planting. They know how much space nature needs. They're patient too. The sun comes out. Suddenly he remembers a moment when he was six or seven, sitting under the apple tree at home. The air was still and sunlight slanted in close to his feet. He dipped a hand into the ray of sun. What he felt was pure joy. He often thinks about this, about this other ideal version of himself he glimpsed that day.

He leaves the main road and turns off into the estate of his client. Mrs Sheridan's car is in the driveway. He has never met Mr Sheridan. Across the street children pedal their bikes along the footpath. He unloads a spade, an electric cutter and cable, a brush, and carries them around to the back of the house. The garden has a deserted feel, even now, with most of the landscaping done. He stands and surveys his work. A curved border runs along three sides of the garden, newly planted with shrubs and climbers. Yesterday he put in a laburnum, and honeysuckle and jasmine against the wall. Today he will finish the planting and set the red paving slabs on the concrete patio. He glances at the back door and then at the upstairs windows. Most days he never sees her.

He digs a hole in the border. He taps out a young fuchsia from its pot. When he lays eyes on the tender nude roots he feels a small twinge between his shoulder blades. He read once in a science magazine that when a tomato is plucked those in the immediate vicinity secrete certain hormones, like the pheromones of fear released by humans in moments of terror. He tries to hold back these thoughts. Sometimes there is too much to take. He left horticultural college because of this, the thought of it all—nature's throb, the secret life of plants, of insects, the hum and frequency of life under the surface. He knew that another reality was within his reach. He was afraid it would break through and he might hear it.

He wheels barrowloads of sand from the front of the house and lays them on the patio, allowing a slight slope towards the garden. He lifts the heavy slabs into place and sets the spirit level on each. The afternoon turns hot and he strips off his sweatshirt.

Inside the house the phone rings. He wonders what she does all day. She never leaves the house. The garden had been bare and forlorn at the start. She left the design and the plant selection entirely up to him. He had the impression that everything, every thought, cost her great effort. On his second day he stood at the back door, poised to knock with a query about the positioning of the wisteria. The door was ajar and he heard her talking on the phone. 'I think so, mmm,' she said, and then in a clear voice, 'I have the patio man here at last. He came yesterday... Yes, he's done that... I was watching him just now from upstairs...'

A while later she brought him out a glass of orange juice.

'Here, take this,' she said and stepped back. He towered over her. She asked about the plants, their names, out of politeness, he thought. He sensed that she longed for him to leave so she could be alone again.

After a moment's silence he nodded towards the garden. 'It's a lovely quiet garden you have. When the plants fill out it'll be very nice.'

'Yes. It will.'

'You could put a bench down in that far corner to catch the sun.'

'Yes, I suppose.'

'You could pave the corner first—there'll be some paving slabs left over.'

'Okay... though I'm not a great one for the outdoors. I don't much like the sun.'

She was very still. He looked into her eyes.

'I prefer winter...' she said. 'So much is expected of people in summer.'

He looked down at the top of her head, at her short dark brown hair. The ends curled out at the nape of her neck.

'I'm not much of a green fingers, I'm afraid,' she said and smiled.

'I can leave you the plan, and gardening books can be very useful.' He mentioned a title. She went inside for a pen and paper and then stood close to him as he spelled out the author's name. Her skin was pale. She was his age or a little older, maybe thirty, and uncertain, as if she wasn't fully sure of her place in that house or garden. As if they weren't really hers. Her arms were bare; she wore a white sleeveless blouse and jeans. She had a mannerism: when she spoke she raised the back of her hand to shield her eyes, and squinted up at him. But the sun wasn't in her eyes. Then, aware of the futility of this gesture, she'd quickly avert her hand to push her hair back. Her hands were a burden to her. Now she gripped the pen tightly with her fingers. They both stood there, looking at the page.

'It's good… very readable,' he said.

She nodded and underlined the title. He noticed a tiny mole above her wrist bone.

'It has a good index.' He felt the silence of the garden close around them.

She drew lines above and below and around the title, boxing it in. They looked down at her boxed words. Their heads were very close. She raised her eyes to his, and let them linger there. Then she walked away.

He remembered how in January he had found a lone flower, a tiny purple Vinca, that had survived the winter under old growth. How, when he pushed aside the weeds, it had astonished him.

The sun is blasting down. He rests for a few minutes. A neighbour's cat walks along the back wall. He hears the far-off murmur of traffic. Sometimes he thinks of going away. He has friends in New York and Boston, working in banks and IT, painting, decorating, gardening too, and fishing on boats off Cape Cod. He looks up and sees the cat watching him. He could always go west—the land is there, it is his. Lately he's been dreaming of warm places. In the bookshops he finds pictures of red-roofed houses on wooded hillsides in Tuscany. There are vineyards and wildflowers and bougainvillea that reminds him of the rhododendrons of Mayo. He thinks of working in such a warm lush place, of how almost anything is possible. But then something—the teemingness of it all—returns to him. Too much abundance, he thinks.

The back door opens and she is standing in the doorway.

'Hello.'

'Hello… You're almost finished, I see.'

'Yeah, another hour should do it, then a bit of tidying up.'

'I have to go out.' He can barely hear her. He takes a step closer.

'Right, okay,' he says.

'I need to pay you but I may not be back when you're leaving. Can you…' She drops something from her hand. She bends slowly and picks up her car keys and as she rises she sways a little.

'Are you okay?'

She takes a step back inside and puts a hand on the counter. He leans into the kitchen. 'Are you not feeling well?'

'No, I need to…' He pulls a chair towards her and she sits down.

'Can I call someone, a doctor?'

'I have to get to the hospital.' She flinches.

He takes out his mobile phone. 'I'll ring an ambulance.'

'No. It would take too long.'

He helps her into her car, then sits in beside her and reverses out of the driveway. She names the hospital, a large, city-centre maternity hospital. He thinks of stories of babies born en route to hospital. This is different. He turns out of the estate. There are speed ramps and he has to slow. When they join the main road she straightens up and leans her head back. He thinks she has come through the worst.

'Traffic isn't too bad this time of day,' he says.

'No.'

A small white dog trots along the footpath.

'Are you feeling better?'

'Yes, I think so. I'm sorry about this.'

'That's okay. No worries.' At a red light a group of teenagers crosses in front of them. The girls have long shiny hair. Halfway across one girl says something, and they all laugh.

'They're lucky, aren't they?' she says. He puts the car in gear and looks at her. Her eyes are green and her hair is tucked behind her ears. Her face is very pale. He glances at her hands.

'Yeah, I suppose,' he says but he isn't sure what she means.

He drives on, stopping and starting in a line of cars. He wonders what lies ahead.

'You're not from the city,' she says then.

'No, I'm from Mayo.'

'On the coast?'

'Yeah.' They are going over the canal bridge now. 'Do you want me to call someone for you when we get there?'

'Yes… No, it's okay, actually. Peter, my husband, is in Germany, on business. I called him already. I have a sister in Meath and she'll come in.'

They are moving very slowly in the traffic.

'Will you go back to Mayo?' she asks. Her face is tilted towards him, calm, serene. He feels himself within her orbit.

'Yes, I think so. I might build a house there.'

'Beside the sea?'

He nods. 'On a hill. Looking out to sea.'

'Oh,' she whispers. She is silent then. Some minutes pass. She has forgotten him. He fears she will fade out and he will lose her.

'Tell me about the place you come from,' she says then.

He shrugs, reluctant.

She lifts her eyes to his face. 'Please.'

'Well, it gets a lot of rain, like everywhere in the west. The roads are bad. The land is poor. But… you get used to all that because it's home, I suppose. I don't know… I only think about my own place, the villages and the towns—Lecanvey and Murrisk and Louisburgh. The Atlantic is always there, pounding away, and the mountains too, Croagh Patrick and Mweelrea, half-hidden in cloud or mist most of the time, but you're always aware of them. And the way people turn to them every day—they don't even know they're doing it. They look out to sea first and then up to the mountain… Sometimes I walk halfway up Croagh Patrick and stand and look out. Then these big clouds come rolling in from the sea and everything changes. You don't know where you are. And the wind—Jesus, it would lift you... On a clear day you can see way out, all the islands in Clew Bay, and Clare Island too. My mother came from Clare Island, she's an island woman...'

He pauses. Her eyes are still on him.

'There's a story she tells,' he says, 'a true story, something that happened in the late eighteen hundreds, I think. It happened on Achill Island... The local people were out working—whole families—in the fields. There was a baby wrapped up asleep in the heather while the mother worked. This huge sea eagle with a seven-foot wingspan flew in, plucked up the sleeping baby in its talons and carried it off out over the sea. All the local men of the island dropped what they were doing and rowed furiously towards Clare Island. The Clare Islanders were alerted too and everyone searched and searched and stretched up into the cliffs and the baby was found, safe and well, asleep in the robber's nest...'

They are weaving their way through the narrow streets near the hospital. Something deep, below words, lies between them.

'Do you know my worst fear?' she asks.

He shakes his head.

'Being alone. Christmases alone by a fire. With maybe a dog or a cat.' She gives a little laugh. Then she leans forward and looks out and up, as if searching the sky for something.

He stops at the hospital entrance and switches off the engine.

'They'll think you're the father,' she says.

Inside she is wheeled away. His final glimpse is of the porter bending down to hear something she's saying. He stands for a few moments in the corridor, his hands hanging by his side.

He walks out of the hospital and gets into the car. He sits there, motionless, with fixed eyes. After a while he pulls away and drives south through the city. His heart is pounding. He glances at the bloodstain on the seat beside him. He remembers her hand raised to shield the sun. He sees her now, lying down, turning to face a wall.

Something had been forming, cell by cell, limb by limb, in the dark of her. Vertebrae, tendon, knucklebone. The iris in an eye. Now, it had fallen away, a subtraction of her being. Fingerprints cut short in the making. He thinks of things he has not thought of before, about women's lives. It is not the same for men at all. His hands turn the steering wheel. His strength, his maleness, is of no avail.

He leaves the main road and turns into her estate. He has the feeling that a long time has passed, years even, and that he will find her garden overgrown and a For Sale sign swinging in the wind. He comes to her house and eases the car into the driveway. He switches off the ignition and listens to the engine ticking. She will be stricken, no longer intact. She might need to touch walls when she gets out. She might not trust the ground anymore. She might slide her foot along the pavement, like a blind person. Trying out the world again.

THIS FALLING SICKNESS

Ruth had not thought of Matt, her first husband, for some time. Then Matt's brother, Paul, called to say he was dead. She was lifting Emily into her cot when the phone rang. A drop of water fell on her head and when she looked up a grey stain had formed on the ceiling. It reminded her of the amoeba in her science book years ago.

'Matt's been killed,' Paul said.

When he said that word, *killed*, for a second Ruth saw him being gunned down in the street. 'He died in Jordan this morning. In a climbing accident.'

He had been with his friend Maurice. The family thought she should know.

'Did Maurice die too?' She was not accustomed to hearing Paul's voice anymore. She stared at the floor and felt herself folding. She thought Matt was behind her, turning a handle, winding her down.

She stood at the bedroom window listening to Emily's wheezing breath and looking down on the garden. The afternoon was grey and very still. In the other house, Matt had laid a gravel path down to the garden shed. Some nights now when she was preparing for bed she would hear Matt's movements below and be surprised by a sudden elation. Then she would catch herself. It was David—

David emptying the dishwasher, opening the back door, putting out the bin. But it was Matt she heard, Matt's step on the stairs, his nighttime movements. As if he had accompanied her into this new marriage. As if he had put his imprint on this new house, this new husband.

The marriage to Matt had lasted ten years. He was older than her, and ready for children from the start. She had not wanted children or anything that might ration her love or alter her indescribable happiness. On all other things they were at one. When Charlie was born a few years later she found that she'd been wrong—that love does indeed beget love. But Matt had not felt the same—he had felt cast aside. He worked long hours and did as he pleased. Her mother told her this was the way with men and babies. It would change when the child got older.

Emily's asthma had become chronic over the winter. Every night her wheeze filled the house and Ruth or David ran up and down the stairs all evening. And yet she slept through the night, this pale compliant child. Charlie had been different—a riotous boy, scarcely sleeping, hyper alert to every sound in the house. She had removed the ticking clock from his room before he was a year old. One Sunday when he was eighteen months, they drove to a restaurant in the foothills of the Dublin Mountains. Charlie followed everything that moved. He spat his dinner down the front of his red jumper and stepped into the path of waiters and around tables, seeking out the children of other diners. Silently, repeatedly, Ruth or Matt went to retrieve him. When they finished Matt paid the bill and Ruth tried to coax Charlie into his buggy. Then her phone rang. It was her sister Angie in London.

From the porch of the restaurant she watched them cross the car park. Matt was holding Charlie with one hand and wheeling the buggy with the other. Every now and then a car whizzed by on the road outside. Matt bent down to fix Charlie's shoe and she saw the pale curls on the back of the child's head rise in the wind. She stepped outside and began the walk to the car. Something was different, something was halted or hovering in the air. On the phone Angie told her she needed to live a little. Matt let Charlie's hand go for a second while he collapsed the buggy and opened the boot. The wind gusted and a strand of hair hit her face and she turned back to catch something Angie was saying. When she turned around Matt was running through the entrance. There was a screech of brakes. She squinted at the red bundle that rose into the air. She watched the falling, so much swifter than the rising, and she was struck by the absurd grace of the movement. She thought that from where Matt was standing, he could have reached out and broken the fall.

Paul called several times during the week with updates on the repatriation of Matt's remains. 'The embassy people are working on it. It's just a matter of waiting now,' he said.

'What happened? Was it a steep fall?'

'No. Just three rises. They had only started out. He lost his foothold—he wasn't roped up.'

She had pictured a great fall, from thousands of feet. From a dazzling white snow field. He had been in thrall to all that, to the colossal silence, to the mysteries of the mountains and their beckoning.

'It was quick,' Paul said. 'He wouldn't have suffered. Maurice had the post-mortem report translated from Arabic today… ' He paused. 'Internal injuries… Do you want to hear this, Ruth?'

His legs had not broken—the long muscular legs he'd thrown across her belly, pinning her down in his sleep, had held firm.

'Are you going out there?' she asked.

'No. Anna thought I should, but Maurice is going to accompany him home. I'll be at the airport and drive west with the hearse.'

At the mention of the hearse she pressed the phone hard against her ear. She had thought he would always exist, and be easily found again. She had not envisaged this. She had not imagined him tumbling from those ancient rocks. She had not foreseen him falling from the sky.

'Ruth,' Paul said, 'I know you have your own life now but—'

'I'll come to the funeral,' she said. Then, 'Is there anyone... A woman, I mean?'

'No. Not that we know of.'

She thought of something. 'Could he have had a heart attack?'

'No. The heart was perfect.'

It was Paul who had driven them to the cemetery that April morning. She and Matt sat in the back with the white coffin on their laps. A small group of mourners was leaving the cemetery and at the sight of the white coffin a woman clasped the arm of another. Ruth kept looking back at them. Then the priest started up the prayers. She heard a tinkle on the wind and she turned her head and there, in row after row, were hundreds of identical graves, each adorned with wind chimes and toys and trinkets, and for a second her heart rose and she turned to tell Matt. But he was leaning into the grave, unsteady with the weight of the coffin in his hands, and her sister was reading a poem in a voice starting to crack. Ruth saw her mother's shoes sinking into the clay and then her brother's startled eyes. The traffic roared just beyond the high wall. Suddenly she was afraid the graves might part, cleave open like the Red Sea and spill out their contents onto the busy road. She closed her eyes for a second and when she opened them her father was leaning against a tree.

The next day they drove back across the city to the cemetery. Matt put his hands in his pockets and circled the grave and looked up at the sky. She tossed little pools of rainwater from the flower wrappings. As they walked away she put her arm through his. The next day he would not go back with her. She pleaded with him. She began to visit alone. She could scarcely conceive of Charlie down there, and when she did she grew afraid. She forced her mind onto other things—the clouds racing across the sky above her, the smooth round stones on the beach near her childhood home, her parents eating breakfast at their kitchen table that morning.

One evening, a few weeks later, Matt came into the kitchen. Her mother and sister had just left and she was standing at the sink washing mugs.

'I'm sorry,' he said.

She turned and looked at him. 'I just want us to go over there together sometimes. Is that too much to ask?'

'No. I mean, I'm sorry it happened. I'm sorry I let go of his hand.'

She turned back to the sink. 'It wasn't your fault.'

A huge bubble formed on the shoulder of her thumb. The face reflected in it was large and distorted. Before it bursts, she thought, he will have left the kitchen.

'It was both our faults,' she said then. 'We never should have had him. I always knew something like this would happen.'

Slowly, with time, people told her, they would recover. Yes, she thought. Matt would come in some evening and she would look up from her book and he would tell her a story from work, and for a few minutes they would return to what they had once been, before he existed. They would not say much at first but by degrees they would start to mention his name. They would survive.

'They should have gone out there to bring him home,' David said. 'If he were my brother, I'd have gone.' He sat on the couch beside her and switched TV channels. She had lain awake the night before, thinking: *We have abandoned you, Matt, we have left you locked in a cold drawer in a foreign land.*

'What time is the flight due?' David asked.

'It's the last Aer Lingus one from Heathrow.'

He brought the Teletext page up on the TV screen and they scanned in silence.

'Due 10pm and it's running forty minutes late already,' he said. 'Jesus, it'll be all hours when they get to Mayo.' He looked at her. 'We can drop Emily off at my mother's on our way.'

She frowned and shook her head. 'You don't need to come.'

She did not want any part of this new life, this second life, touching the first. 'Please, I'm asking you,' she said.

'Why do you have to go at all? What good will it do?'

He turned away, hurt. The nine o'clock news ended. The weather came on. The next day would be dry and sunny, with heavy rain moving eastwards in the evening. She looked at the map of Ireland on the screen. The damp Mayo soil was already piled up beside the open grave.

'I'll make us tea,' David said.

They sat on the couch with tea and biscuits. David tracked the flight obsessively. Finally, at 11.48pm, it landed.

'Go to bed now,' he said softly.

The year after Charlie's death they had rented a cottage on an island off Mayo. It was March and they slept late and woke to the sound of the sea and the white light in the bedroom. By day they walked around the island, over sand dunes, in and out of little inlets and across tiny pristine beaches, as if they were the first humans to set foot on those sands. On the mainland they climbed Croagh Patrick and the clouds parted and he pointed out their island in Clew Bay. That evening a fisherman took their photograph on the pier. Matt had his arm around her shoulder and her hair was blown back by the wind. Minutes later he stripped off his clothes and swam out with the tide. Her eyes never left him. She remembered a hike he'd taken her on, years before, on the Wicklow Mountains. They had walked all day and he had held her hand crossing streams. When they got to the highest peak he stood behind her with his breath on her cheek and stretched out his arm as if he had conjured up the whole view, the whole mountain range, especially for her. As if to say, *See, you might have your books, but look, look at what I can give you.*

She stood on the pier until he swam back in. That night in the cottage, with the lamps lit and the radio on, they cooked a long slow meal and drank wine and listened to the waves crashing on the rocks. She had not thought of the child for hours. She closed her eyes for a second. *We are here, now,* she thought. *We have come through it.*

Emily woke that night, crying. David lifted her into their bed. Water dripped from the ceiling into a bucket. It was 3am, the dead of night. The hearse was moving across the country, its headlights cutting a tunnel through the dark. Soon it would round a bend and the dark bulk of Croagh Patrick would loom over it.

'Sleep,' David whispered. 'Sleep... It will all be over tomorrow.'

She listened for the plop of each drop in the bucket. She knew now that Matt's stamp on her was permanent. She dozed off and fell into a dream. A phone was ringing in an empty house. It rang for a long time and when she picked up, it was Matt, calling from abroad. There was static on the line, followed by little blips, like Morse code. Then his voice broke through. 'Guess who died?' he said.

The weather held all day. In the church the priest said Matt's name over and over. Paul read from the Scriptures and a fiddler played a slow air. In the front pew his mother and sisters sat still and upright. Behind them Paul, with a back like Matt's, sat next to his wife Anna and their teenage sons. The coffin of Lebanese cedar was ten feet away. She could feel his closed eyes watching her. A shaft of sunlight fell through a high window and hit the head of the priest, and dust particles floated down from the raised Host. She tilted her head, and followed the slanting ray of sun, and a memory rushed in of a day—an evening—in autumn, eighteen months after Charlie's death. Some instinct had prompted her to take a walk, and down the street, the sun disappeared and she felt drops of rain on her head, but forced herself on, because every small triumph counted in those days. But then the drops came heavier and she turned and hurried back to the house. At the front window she stood for a moment and looked in. He was sitting on the couch talking on the phone, and just the sight of him restored her. Then she tapped the glass with her fingernail to startle him—no, surprise him—with her unexpected return. He jumped up in panic and dropped the phone into its cradle. She stepped back onto the grass and crushed a snail underfoot.

'Who were you calling?'

'No one. I wasn't calling anyone.' She saw the gold flecks in his eyes and they were jumping.

When he went out she pressed the redial button. A woman answered, 'Hello.' And again, 'Hello.' In the background there were children, a TV, a kitchen maybe. Ruth hung up and redialled and the woman on the other end was silent.

There were other signs too, that made her insides quicken, and eventually she knew he wanted to be found out. He showed no remorse. She, Ruth, had grown distant. He had felt her silent blame every day—with her dead eyes she had accused him. For months she did nothing—she could not countenance being without him. Then, when the woman in the kitchen began to call and calmly ask for him by name, Ruth left.

The congregation stood and there was a rattle of chains, and a cloud of incense rose to the roof. The coffin was wheeled outside and they walked behind it down the hill to the graveyard. Was it Solomon's chariot that was fashioned from cedar wood? Was it the cedars of Lebanon that wept? She pictured his house back in the city—bills on the table, dishes in the sink, his bike in the hall. She thought his death had imperilled her, too. She thought how its timing had hovered over him, hidden from him. How he had risen each morning for weeks, months, years and moved through each day and lain down each night, but the countdown had begun—he was already hurtling towards this moment, as she was towards hers.

Flocks of seagulls circled and shrieked above the grave as the mourners gathered close. The waves lapped on the shore and the murmur of the Rosary rose and fell and enclosed her. Across the open grave Paul's head was bowed, a son on either side of him. She closed her eyes. She should not have come. She should not have listened out for Matt's echo, or let him summon her here like this.

In the distance the church bell rang and she looked up and saw Anna with tears slipping down her face, and she was thrown. Their eyes met and lingered for a second, and Ruth, feeling herself weaken, searched Anna's face for a moment and then the face of the woman next to her, and then slowly, abstractedly, face by face, other random women in the crowd. She might be here, she thought, the woman in the kitchen with the TV on, might be here. I might have always known her. I might have walked down the hill beside her now. She peered at each woman's face. *Is it you?* she mouthed across the grave. *Or you? Or you?*

And then something on the edge of Anna moved. Her son's arm dropped by his side. Ruth shifted her gaze to his face. Paul Junior, the second son. He had been a small boy when she knew him, seven or eight, no more. Now he had the thin face and raw features of a mid-teen, before the bones are properly scored or perfected. He is still in the making, she thought—and she began to study his face and eyes and body for some resemblance to Matt, or for how the child might one day have looked, or borne himself. The boy was staring straight ahead. Then his eyelids flickered and his eyes rolled back, and a damp patch appeared and spread down the front of his trousers. He fell to the ground heavily and his head hit the edge of the grave. Paul and Anna dropped to their knees beside him and the priest stumbled in his prayer and paused. And then the boy's limbs stiffened and jerked and his whole body began to vibrate. His teeth clenched and his face beat against the clay. Paul half-stood and signalled to the priest—a look of reassurance and a plea to continue. Then he bent and laid a hand on his son's convulsing back, and waited. A hush descended on the mourners and the priest's words were barely audible. The boy's body shook and thrashed and Ruth stood paralysed, caught in its hazard, as if wired to the boy and his tender taut brain, as if the neurons that misfired and hurled through him were escaping and crossing and alighting on her and she, too, would be felled in this neurological strike.

Then the storm passed. The thrashing eased and his limbs slowly stilled. Ruth held her breath. For a few seconds all was quiet and she felt a part of her shift, lighten, enter a new dimension. She had a vague sensation of Matt's nearness. She saw the boy, foetal, on the ground. His completion had been interrupted, logic and memory momentarily wiped out. Scorch marks left on a delicate cerebral membrane. He opened his eyes and raised his head and Paul and Anna lifted him up and he stood pale, dazed, resurrected. The crowd stepped back and the three of them, stooped and leaning into each other like one body, sleepwalked away.

The mourners closed in and the priest started up again. Out on the road she glimpsed Paul open a car door. She imagined the three of them in the back seat, Paul Junior in the middle, a hand from each side touching him, earthing him again. His absence now left her more deeply alone. The priest intoned the prayers and the mourners responded louder and harder than ever, and the coffin was lowered into the grave. She watched it disappear. Her only link to the child was going too. *Holy Mary, Mother of God, pray for us sinners.* The volume shocked her. *Now and at the hour.* A day would come when there would be no trace of Matt left, either. Clods of earth fell on the lid and she looked up at the sky and became, suddenly, bereft. Once, their eyes had ached for each other. Their hearts had chimed. In one another's silence they had known joy and loneliness, in equal measure. In the end he had accelerated away from the reach of grief, and from his own unfathomable self. What he had done, his betrayal, was not unforgiveable. She knew then it was easier to be the one hurt, than the hurter.

Strangers reached out and embraced her and strong hands gripped hers, and there was no escape. She wished the heavens would open and drive the mourners back to their cars. She wanted to flee the graveyard and find their island out in the bay and run all day over the long grass and the dunes until she reached the pristine beach with the immaculate sands. There she would lie down in the dark. She would whisper his name to the sands; she would tell him there is no giving like the first giving, that what is given first cannot be regiven, what is first taken cannot be retaken. She would tell him she would never be the same again, or give the same or receive the same or love the same, that it was in him that all possibilities were first encountered, all beauty, all hope concentrated, that he had gone now and taken something and it could not be recovered and she was left here, now, impaired, diminished, she was left wanting.

In the evening rain swept in from the Atlantic. She left Mayo and drove east through the dark. The lights of oncoming cars began to dazzle. She pulled over onto the hard shoulder and stared out the window. She would see him everywhere falling. The wipers thumped back and forth. They are all dying, she thought, the males are all dying around me.

She edged back out into the traffic. It does not matter, she thought, what can one do? She imagined the car as a tiny dot on the map of Ireland, crawling across its centre, and behind, moving further and further away, Mayo, the black night and the rain seeping down, dampening and darkening the clay, the stones, the grain of the wood.

SLEEPING WITH A STRANGER

He left behind the warm waters of the bay, the seaweed, the blue of the Burren. He swam in a current of his own and hovered, like a skydiver in the dark. He would swim out far, underwater, to the Continental Shelf. He no longer felt man, but marine. He had a need to reach the depths, to glide to the silent darkness and feel the cold brush of luminous sea creatures.

When he came up for air he was blinded by the sun. He turned his head and saw the yellow diving platform and the concrete roof of the changing shelter, saw that he had barely moved beyond the rocks. In the distance the sun glinted on a car roof moving along the Prom. He swam back in and hoisted himself up onto the path, dripping seawater, his body tight and sinewy and vigorous again.

It was October. The morning was bright, cold. In the shelter he dressed and wrung out his swimming trunks. He combed his hair and felt himself coming back to the world. Mona would be in the kitchen at that moment, clearing away the breakfast things. In a while she would leave the house and take the Knocknacarra bus into town for her Saturday morning coffee and then, later, lunch with friends. He took his bag and began the walk to his car. He felt a slight uncertainty since leaving the water, as if the day was not to be trusted. A woman in dark clothes and long hair walked ahead of him, looking out to sea. He turned his head to the same angle and followed a wave until it merged with the grey water in the bay. As he drew close to the woman he felt a faint quickening. He came level and turned his face to hers. Their eyes met and she looked away quickly. She was not who he thought she was.

Mona had left a note on the counter to say she'd be gone all day. She and her friends—all teachers—would linger over lunch and wine and talk of school and family, and the longing for retirement. Mona kept herself well and looked a decade younger than her sixty years. She read novels and played bridge and together they went to the theatre and concerts and occasionally had friends over for dinner. He poured a glass of water and sat at the table, the house silent around him. He licked his forearm and tasted salt and remembered when he was a child how his father placed mineral licks in fields and sheds to ease the craving in calves. They might dement themselves licking the rungs of gates otherwise. He looked around the kitchen, delaying the moment when he would go upstairs to his desk and sift through notes and begin his report on a whole-school evaluation he'd completed that week. He no longer cared for his work. He would like to be devoted to one thing but had never found that thing. He looked out the window. They had lived in this house for twenty-eight years. Mona was a twin and one night in bed she spoke into the dark. 'If I ever die, you must marry my sister,' and he swore that he would, that he would seek out only those bearing the greatest likeness to her. It had felt like a pact. But she did not die and her sister went to Australia. One morning, soon after, she walked into the kitchen and stood in a pool of light under the yellow cabinets and told him she was pregnant. They had children because they could not be childless; childlessness would have magnified the loneliness of marriage.

In mid-morning the nursing home in Athlone called to report on his mother's condition. She had Alzheimer's and had been winding down for years and now there was cause for concern. He drove east out of the city on the new motorway. He had driven the roads of the county for twenty-five years as a primary schools' inspector, heading deep into the countryside each morning, past fields with stone walls, and cows being driven home for milking, through sleepy villages an hour before anyone rose. In late spring sheep huddled behind walls, bleating for their lambs, and the lambs, newly weaned, cried out their own terrible lament from nearby sheds. Once, he stopped and stood on the raised verge of the roadside looking over a wall at them, listening to their plaintive bleating. He sat into his car and drove on. How long, he wondered, before the ache of a ewe disappears?

He looked at the land beyond the motorway, at a tree on a hill, a cow, the dome of the sky. He wondered about the existence of these things—a tree, an animal, an insect. He wondered if theirs was any greater, any happier, than his own. He would have liked to talk about these things but it was too late now. He could not broach such things with Mona. They had not made love in a year. He remembered the woman on the Prom earlier, gazing out to sea like the woman at the end of a pier in a film he'd once seen. He saw lone women everywhere. One morning over twenty years ago he had passed a helmeted girl on the roadside. Her motor bike was parked and she was leaning over a dead fox. A few miles further on he arrived at the local school and as he walked up the path with the principal, the girl arrived and he turned and saw her unzip her jacket and remove the helmet and shake her hair free. Her name was Grace. He sat under a map of Ireland at the back of the classroom, observing her. He listened as she told the children that she had passed a dead body on the road. She had touched it, she said, and it was warm. A family of cubs would go hungry that day. All morning she moved among the children and bent her head close to theirs and whispered in their ears. Sometimes she smiled at him and they exchanged little knowing looks. She wore jeans and a white shirt. Her limbs were young, strong, unscarred, her body with its whole sensual life before it. He said her name in Irish,

Gráinne, and at the end of the lesson he asked, What did you want to be when you were small? I wanted to be everything, she said.

Mona would be in the restaurant by now, settling herself in her seat, lifting out her reading glasses to study the menu. She was not without her mystery. She had a bridge partner, a school colleague named Tim. He thought of them at the card table at night, and the looks that must pass between them. He remembered once watching a TV programme about rock climbing, and how climbing partners grow to read each other's minds, to comprehend each other in some deep silent way. Their lives depend on one another.

In the nursing home his mother's mouth was open, like the little beak of a fledgling. Sometimes on his visits a terrified look would cross her face when he entered her room. He said her name, Mother. Her frame was shrunken and the veins and arteries were visible on the undersides of her arms. Her slippers sat neatly on the floor by the radiator. A nurse came and stood beside him and spoke softly. 'The doctor saw her earlier. Her lungs are not good… he doesn't think there's much time left.' He felt his mother's hand. When his father lay dying, his hands and feet and nose, the extremities, had grown gradually colder. His mother had kept touching them, as if temperature, and not hours or minutes, was the measure of time. Soon after his death she herself began to fade. She filled the electric kettle with milk and was frightened by rain. She began to sing the songs of Jeanette MacDonald and Nelson Eddy. She remembered what he had just said, but not the thing before. He thought of her brain as being littered with a hail of tiny holes, like the spread of buckshot.

That spring, years ago, he found excuses to revisit the girl in the classroom. He was touched by her youth and her sympathy. He hoarded up thoughts of her and as he drove home, he let them suffuse him. He would remember her little cough, or the way she forgot he was there and absent-mindedly put her head in her hands at her desk. On the final observation day he sat at the back of her class again, drafting his official report. When he looked up, her eyes were on him, unsmiling, looking deeply into him.

At the end of the day, with the pupils dismissed, he invited her to sit.

'You have a bright future ahead of you,' he said.

'Thank you.'

'This job is temporary. Jobs are scarce. Do you have something else lined up?'

She gave a slight shrug. 'No, not really. I'm going to Dublin for the summer. A few us are taking a house there, we're going to try some street theatre.'

He smiled and indicated that she should continue.

'I don't know if we'll even survive. We have high hopes! We'll probably be forced back into the classroom in September.' Her eyes were green. Her neck was smooth and white. 'Long term, though, we'll probably go to America.'

He cleared his throat, and moved his papers about. 'Really? To teach?'

She tilted her head a little. 'Mmm, I don't know… maybe… I want to go to New York for a while, hang out there, you know, live through four seasons in the city.' Her eyes were lit up. 'Anyway if I do go it'll be with the gang. There's a community drama programme we're hoping to get onto. America's great for that kind of thing. I had a job there last summer. The people are different, they're very… trusting. I met a poet at a bus stop one day… he talked to me like he knew me my whole life.'

Under the cuffs of her shirt her wrists were white and narrow. He had a glimpse of her future. She would hear the cries of men and children.

'So you're off to the Big Apple for a wild time then!'

'Oh, I wouldn't say that, I wouldn't say "wild". I don't even drink.'

'No?'

'No. Don't get me wrong. I used to. I just don't like what it can do.'

Suddenly he felt reckless. 'What can it do?'

She blew out slowly and her fringe lifted in the stream of air. 'Well… I'd be afraid of losing control. I might end up falling down on the street… getting run over by a bus… sleeping with a stranger.'

Down the corridor a door slammed. Then there was silence. He thought she might hear the terrible commotion inside him. He picked up the report and handed it to her. 'I don't usually do this,' he said.

She read the page silently and then left it down in front of him. 'Thank you,' she said in a whisper.

He began to tidy his papers. His hands were trembling. He was aware of time slipping violently by.

'There's a job coming up in a school not far from here… ' He could not look at her so he leaned down for his bag. 'I know the principal, he's a friend… if you were interested…' He searched for the right words. 'You'd be a great asset to the school.'

They looked at each other. He saw her absorb the implications of the offer, and then her eyes softened with too much understanding and it was unbearable.

'Of course, you may not want to stay around,' he said. 'From what you've said…'

He had almost lost the run of himself. He had become a small raw thing.

'Well… thank you. But if I do stick with teaching it'll probably be in Dublin.'

Driving back to the city that evening he grew distraught. Mona would never know the depths of him. He would die a faithful husband. They were bound together by the flesh of three sons and the dread of loneliness. That night he stood before a mirror. He thought he could hear the sound of his pulse fading. Every morning after that, at every daybreak, something slipped away. He drove along city streets in the evenings and stared at the backs of girls and women. Her name, her face, hovered behind his eyes. He went down to the strand on summer nights with the city lights at his back and stripped off and rolled out with the waves. He worked long hours and drove his sons hard at their studies and sports and exhausted everyone around him, and some days Mona turned on him with bitter, baffled eyes and he knew then they had passed some milestone and there was no turning back.

His mother did not open her eyes. He drew the window blind down halfway, and waited. She lay supine before him, the torso, the bones that had borne the freight of her life, sunken in the bed. A girl with a plain wide face carried in a lunch tray and he smiled weakly and shook his head. She returned a few minutes later and, without a word, placed a cup of tea and two biscuits in front of him. This simple act moved him greatly.

In the late afternoon he walked outside and sat on a wooden bench and texted Mona. He dialled his sister's number and then instantly cancelled it. He wanted the day, and the death if it occurred, to himself. He walked around the back and stood on the edge of the lawn looking down at the Shannon. Pleasure cruisers were tied up at a small marina on the far side. Further along the bank there was a new hotel, like a large white cube. The water was calm; the reeds made the river patient. He leaned against a tree and looked up at the steel railway bridge high above the river. Just then the Dublin train nosed into view and crossed the bridge, and, out of the blue, he remembered Grace again.

He had come upon her, unexpectedly, just three years before, when he had been addressing a teachers' conference in Maynooth. The crowd was large and during the morning coffee break, he turned to leave his empty cup on the long table and there she

73

stood, no more than four feet away, calmly considering him. They were instantly recognisable to each other. Her hair was longer, darker, with a stripe of grey at the front, like a badger's. The stripe marked her out as different, changed, afflicted. *We are the same now,* he thought, *you have caught up.*

'I am forty,' she said, 'and married.' She crossed her hands on her lap. A great happiness had entered him the moment she sat into his car. He could not explain the closeness he felt to her. He was driving towards the city, blind, resolute. He thought of all the car journeys, all the years of remembrance. They floated along the quays in the late afternoon sun. He drove into an underground car park and they climbed concrete stairs and when they emerged out onto the street she let him take her hand. They entered a hotel, and up in the room he stood at the window and looked down at the street. Then he turned and crossed the floor and laid his head on her lap. They did not speak. He felt like a man in a novel—silent, obsessed, extreme in his love. He thought of this moment as his last chance, his only chance, and he felt everything—the past, the future—become almost obliterated by it.

'Tell me your life,' he whispered. The room was still warm from the day's heat. Soon, outside, the light would fade.

She smiled. 'A man broke my heart, once,' she said quietly.

'Your husband?'

'No. Another man. In America… an actor. I met my husband when I came back.' She gave a little laugh. 'He insists on loving me… I will never have children.'

'I'm sorry.'

She stroked his hair.

'Did you get over him? The American guy?'

She looked past him. 'When I came back I stayed at my mother's. I used to walk the lanes. It was summer then. One evening I took her car and drove for miles. When I returned I parked in the local churchyard, at the back, under the yew trees. I thought, This is where people come on summer evenings to do away with themselves. But I just sat there. I was so pierced... I thought we were predestined.'

She took his hand and led him to the bed. She removed his shoes. The charge was immense. The light in the room had changed and he was reminded of midsummer evenings in childhood when daylight vanished and a certain kind of sadness fell on him. She raised her face to him, her throat, the tender place on her temple that he wanted to touch. He saw her eyes, saw that something in her had been extinguished. Who did this to you? he wanted to say. He took her in his arms and covered her with his whole body, with the soles of his feet. 'Go deep,' she whispered.

They lay side by side looking up at the ceiling. He heard the rumble of the city in the distance. She had made him feel vast. He had to hold back words, thoughts, search for other words that might bear their weight. He remembered something from the radio that day, about how the skies are full of old junk, thousands of space shuttles and old Russian satellites that are breaking up and falling to earth as debris. Pieces the size of a family car could come crashing down on one's house. He turned to tell her this. Her eyes were on him, full and moist and desolate.

'He only liked the beginnings of things,' she whispered. 'He used to hit me... He was so broken. It made me love him more.'

Twilight came. He had an urge to carry her to the car and drive off with her. Gradually, beside him, he felt her grow remote. She stepped from beneath the sheet and crossed the room. The light came on in the bathroom and the door closed softly. Then the shower was running. He looked at the shapes in the room, the TV screen, the lamps, the armchairs. He waited a long time. He knew then that she wanted him gone. He rose and dressed and went down in the lift, his legs barely able to ferry him. Out in the evening he felt sick in his stomach. The orange streetlights made everything eerie. He drove along empty streets where the trees hung low. He did not know his way out of the city. He stopped and sat in a café under harsh lights and stared at his reflection in the plate-glass window. He thought of her back in the hotel room, sitting in front of the mirror, brushing her hair in long, even strokes.

The horizon turned black as he drove west. He imagined forks of lightning striking the road, lighting up the way ahead. He opened the window and cold air streamed in and he accelerated hard and closed his eyes for a few seconds. It did not matter if he never reached home. He knew what awaited him, what had to be got through. He knew the water in the bay and every city street and every tree on his road. He knew his own driveway and the front door where his key fitted and the sound of his step on the stairs and the smell of the warm sheets rising to meet him. He pictured himself sitting on the edge of the bed, his weight sagging as he bent down and took off his shoes. He thought how such small things—untying shoelaces, undressing—or the thought of such things, could unhinge a man.

Lights were coming up across the river, on the marina, in the hotel, and soon they would rise from the town and reflect on the water. He felt a little chill. He crossed the damp grass and went inside. They had put a small table in his mother's room, with a white cloth and a crucifix and two lighted candles. He listened to his mother's breath, shortening. He laid his fingers on her pulse and rested them there and felt himself weaken in a moment of terrible tenderness, of mercy. He felt it in his arms, *caritas*, a love for her greater now than at any moment in his whole life. Suddenly, she opened her eyes wide and stared, frightened, at something at the foot of the bed. He whispered *Momma*, and moved to that spot and for one long beautiful moment he thought she was back, that it was all a mistake and in the next moment she would sit up and be whole again, and elated. But her eyes looked through him, seeing something beyond him.

The building was quiet. He thought he should whisper something in her ear. Her lungs were rattling, filling up with liquid. Soon they would be full. When it happened, when the moment arrived, her little breaths petered out in one long exhalation, and he held his own until it ceased.

He sat there for a long time feeling it was neither day nor night. Something remained, drifting in the room. She had been long gone before tonight, long exiled. He had lived in an exile of his own too, in recent years. He closed his eyes now. Mona had made his home. She had made his children, inside her. He turned his head to where his mother's slippers sat on the floor. The sight of them, their patient waiting, moved him. He bent down and took them on his lap and put a hand inside each one. His heart began to pound. He had given Mona the whole of his life, the days, the hours, the quotidian. Every single day, but one. She would have him beyond this life too. Their bones would lie in the same grave and lean against each other and calcify in the earth together. What more could she want? What more could he give?

He was still for a long time. He did not know if this moment counted for everything or almost nothing. He drove west into the night. On the radio a piano was playing, single high notes, marvellous and pure, like the ringing of delicate bells. Their tinkle, their ambulation, tapped on his soul and made it soar.

AND WHO WILL PAY CHARON?

Last summer I heard she was out. She was seen down by the lake late in the evenings, her grey hair down to her backside. Or coming out of the local shop with her groceries in a cloth bag, her eyes cast down as she pushed her bicycle out of the village. She spoke to no one. Though I pictured her standing at the shop counter pointing a finger and saying *loaf*, *tea* in an abrupt voice, then thrusting a twenty-euro note at the shopkeeper in an outstretched hand.

One evening I drove over by the lake and parked in the pub car park. I thought I might glimpse her head bobbing above the hedge on the lane leading down to the water. The place is popular with anglers, and as I waited a couple of Englishmen strolled up the lane, opened their jeeps, lifted in their catch. When the light began to fade I drove away.

After forty years hidden from view she had become a curiosity to the locals, to me too. I imagined her leaning in over the lake, gazing at her green watery reflection, her long hair breaking the surface. I drove by her house that evening. There was no sign of life. I turned the car around and just past the bend I saw the figure up ahead on foot, crossing the road from the lane, bearing down on a bicycle. I slowed down and we looked at each other. Her face was white, her cheeks hollow. I let down the window and she came close up to the car and wiped her mouth roughly with the back of her hand. Her eyes narrowed. Then, with a bewildered look, she jerked her head away fiercely and scurried off. I stared in the rear-view mirror after her. I knew she had not forgotten me.

'Claude… That's a strange name for around here,' she said. It was late and we were sitting on a low wall outside the dancehall in the local town. Her hair was dark and silken. She had just qualified as a nurse.

'I'm not from around here,' I said. 'I'm from Dublin. But my mother was from Kilcash. I'm staying over there with my aunt.'

I watched her take this in. I had noticed how country people—even the staff in the boys' boarding school where I had come to teach—treated me with a little reserve, reverence even, when I said I was from Dublin.

'And who called you Claude, if your mother was from Kilcash?' she asked.

'My father's name was Claude. He's dead now. He was a Protestant. He had to convert to marry my mother.'

She was quiet then. Perhaps she was thinking what I had thought as a child—that my father must have loved my mother greatly to have crossed over.

'It's not as drastic as it sounds,' I said. 'He wasn't religious. Protestants aren't glued to their religion like us Catholics.'

I saw relief in her eyes. So it wasn't the idea of my father's sacrifice for love that had silenced her before, but worry that I too might be a Protestant. 'And you, *Suzanne*? Why aren't you a Mary or a Margaret or an Ann?'

She smiled. 'My mother had an aunt, a nun. She spent a few years in a convent in France—near Limoges, where the famous china comes from. There was a young novice there called Suzanne. She'd arrived at the convent gates one evening after walking for miles, and the nuns took her in. She was an orphan. She saw terrible things in her young life—I don't know what, maybe the war. Anyway my mother said if she ever had a daughter she'd call her Suzanne. And she did. But then Suzanne died when she was a year old, and a few years later she had me. I suppose she didn't want to waste the name.'

Our names, in this place, had bound us. We were a little apart, she hauling the dead sister around, me with the Protestant blood in my veins. We spent evenings together. She told me her mother could be severe on people, even on her. One day we took the train to Dublin. She was very shy at the start. We went out to Howth and walked along the pier and then up the hill. I told her about Yeats and Maud Gonne and the day in 1892 when they cycled out there from the city.

'They went out to visit Maud's aunt, or some relative,' I said. 'They walked along the sea cliffs. Afterwards Yeats wrote a poem, "The White Birds", about that day.' I did not say that the poem held the wish that the two lovers be together forever, like the seagulls. I was not sure what I felt. I had nothing to pit the day against, no past loves. We walked around the city. In a pub, in a moment of joy and brief forgetfulness, she put a hand out to touch my arm and then, remembering herself, she shrank back swiftly, painfully, as if stung. It was this nervousness and her nearness that moved me. Nothing more. That day a huge Irish wolfhound had come towards us on the pier and in panic she'd crossed to my other side. I should have taken her hand. I saw how easily she was shaken—startled by the train's sudden jolting or by car horns or cries on the streets. On the way home the train slowed and stopped in the middle of nowhere and in the eerie quiet of the carriage she looked out at a dark forest. I felt a wave of tenderness for her, for the part of her that so feared the world.

What came to mind in that moment were afternoons at university with my head full of Homer, sitting next to a fellow student in Greek Studies, and being briefly, easily, understood.

I wanted to want her that day in Howth, and other days. I wanted to charge our moments with romance. But as soon as she

81

showed any sign of closeness or keenness or intimacy—even the mention of a next meeting—I withdrew in sullen silence.

One February night she came to my aunt's door. 'I'm going away,' she said. Her voice was strained. 'I have a job offer in London.' My heart gave a little flutter. I felt such relief. 'Unless you want me to stay,' she added.

That evening last summer after meeting her on the road I came home and opened a bottle of wine and let *The Köln Concert* fill the house at high volume. When Jarrett began the climb in the first movement, I felt each pensive note brush my thoughts, I felt him pluck silence from inside me and put notes on it, put an act of faith in it. It was the same quiet collapse I'd felt on first hearing it thirty years ago. The notes rose and swelled and then fell away in that beautiful mesmeric descent. All my life music and books have been the refuge of my mind, the means of striving towards something pure and absolute and sublime. But how can I know what poets and musicians know? They suffer. They feel deeply. They weep for parched sparrows. And for some every angel is indeed terrible. Once I read a story about a woman whose job it was to care for an old bedridden man. The old guy still craved physical intimacy, and one day, moved with compassion, she locked the door and took off her top and let him fondle her breasts. There are some people for whom one will give almost anything and tolerate almost anything because of what they have suffered, because of the high order of their souls.

Over the years, over long winters and occasional melancholic nights I would often think 'How bad could it have been, marriage?' Other men manage. It would have brought its comforts—a family in whom to hope, a wife to direct a man outwards. Then I would find myself behind a woman in a queue and my eyes would fasten on her heavy arms or on flesh bulging over a band of her clothing and I'd feel a small jab at the base of my spine. Or I'd see a local couple drive by on a Sunday afternoon, the back seat full of kids, a wife in the front, and in the man's face a glimpse of the cloying nature of domesticity. I'd turn in my gate, open my door, enter my quiet sheltered life with astonishing relief. She sent me a card that first Christmas, her address on the left-hand side, and a PS underneath. *If we're good, we'll keep.* They did not sound like her words, but I knew what it took for her to write them.

A year after she left, in springtime, my aunt suffered a stroke and was dead by the following autumn. She left me her house and it was the local builder whom I'd hired to do renovations over a year later who told me of Suzanne's return. He was building a house for Tom Cleary, he said. 'I believe the sister is back from England.' He must have seen something in my face or known of my connection. 'Did you not hear? Oh she's back a while now but no one has laid eyes on her—she doesn't go out or go to Mass or anything, and if you ever called up there there'd be all this shuffling and whispering and running around inside before they'd answer the door. The mother doesn't let on that the daughter is back. In fairness, the brother is a nice fellow… She was a nurse in London, I believe.'

That winter I saw something that knocked me sideways. One morning in the dark I was awoken by a strange prompting. Something drew me outside. The world was encased in frost. I walked along the road and up the hill and into a field. My breath came in little bursts of vapour. I walked deep into the fields and there, ahead of me, rose a colossal ghostly silhouette. Horses… seven, eight of them, standing still and silent. Even when I drew close they did not stir. They looked at me and I at them, in perfect accord. Then the sky lightened and a ray of sun broke through and blazed on the horizon and steam rose from the horses' backs and their coats shone. Still they looked at me, with dark patient eyes. I have never felt such wholeness, such oneness.

No, that is not correct. There was an afternoon long ago at

university, with the sun slanting in through high windows and beside me, in the seat next to me, a pale youth from the west of Ireland, with fair to reddish hair and delicate cheekbones and tired misty eyes. Whenever he spoke he cast his eyes down, and his eyelids flickered. I would see him in the refectory among loud youths from the country, and I had an impulse to say, *They are not your kind*. His hand lay on the desk inches from mine that day. Something tender and unsayable lay there too. Perhaps it was the intensity of the Greek discourse, the tragic heroes and their reliance on the gods, and a wish on my part to inhale everything pure and radiant and divine then, but his presence and the still dreamy air of that afternoon filled me with a great upflow of joy, of benevolence for all of mankind.

For a while, forty years ago, Suzanne's return subverted my thoughts. I suspected a child, given up in England—or maybe even kept and concealed there in the house with the mother's collusion. Such things happen. No one saw anything and gradually, over the years, people forgot and the story faded. I forgot too or doubted that she was ever inside that house. Years later when her mother died she still did not come out. Her brother delivered provisions to her door. Then, following a long illness, my own mother died in Dublin. Sometimes, feeling guilty that my grief was not greater, I would drive over by the lake at night and find myself approaching Suzanne's house. What did I expect—that I would come upon her taking the night air too, or out walking a large odd-looking child on a lead under the stars? I remember the moon, its thin fragile crescent hanging delicately over her house. I walked down to the lake's edge one night and let the water lap at my feet. I am not certain there was feeling in my heart for anyone—for my dead mother, for Suzanne, even for myself. I had my life, tight and contained, and few regrets. I drove to school every day, attended to my teaching duties, hoping—particularly in the early years—that

84

my teaching duties, hoping—particularly in the early years—that something, Homer perhaps, might affect the boys and alter their lives. I came home in the evenings and listened to music and cooked and read late into the night. In summer I took trips—Athens, Vienna, Bayreuth. Little, apart from the odd metaphysical ache, ever caused a ripple on this composed life. Occasionally, moments in the classroom when I'd be pulled up by a line or an answer or an insight from a boy. Moved by a recitation of Socrates' speech from the dock, or Achilles' lament for great-hearted Patroclus. Such pitiable things. Once, after a morning considering Orpheus, I read aloud from Rilke's sonnet and there, standing on the raised dais in my classroom, I came briefly undone. I was hearing the notes of Orpheus's lyre, seeing his anxious head glance back and glimpse Eurydice, feeling his bereftness as he ascended the underworld without her. *She's dead*, Hades said, *You cannot have her back.*

Last year I retired. I do not know where the years have gone. I do not know, either, what difference, if any, I ever made to a boy's life. There were, over the years, a few whose sensibilities, whose casts of mind, were similar to my own, yet I never felt compelled to follow their progress or career paths. Perhaps I was afraid I might see in these boys my own unborn sons. I must have known I would never engender life like other men. That the nearest sires I would have would be those boys in the desks before me, the only offspring the gods and goddesses pressing forth from the pages, needing delivery. On weekend visits to my mother in the early years I would occasionally run into old school and college friends in the city, with a child or two in tow, and I would smile and admire the children and enquire after their lives. One day in a bookshop a college classmate asked if I'd heard about Cóilín McDonagh. My eyes might have narrowed a little at the name, I might have had a brief intake of breath, bracing myself for news of me that somewhere on the west coast of America, Cóilín had crashed his motorcycle into a tree and been killed instantly. As he spoke I was staring at the spine of a book behind his head, and thinking of palm trees and ocean swells and open-topped cars on a Pacific highway. And fine cheekbones being smashed against a redwood. I think now that leaving university was my first real encounter with grief. A sickly unease in those final weeks, a paralysis, a constriction of the heart at the prospect of parting. But what could be done? What could be said? There was no call for farewells.

I am determined to travel more. Last month I went to Berlin. The Middle East—Jerusalem—calls to me. I picture myself, a contrary old atheist, moving along the narrow alleys of the city, stopping to talk to old men in doorways—Jew, Christian and Muslim alike— curious to glean something ancient and abiding in their faith and catch a glimpse of the God gene that has bypassed me or lies inert within me. Lately I am intrigued by genes, by the randomness of genes, the randomness of any gene being switched on or off, and how that determines what we are, what makes us one thing or another.

These were my thoughts driving home from the airport last month. As I neared the village I drew up at the T-junction and yielded. A slow-moving hearse drifted into view and passed before my eyes, heading towards the cemetery. Half a dozen cars crawled behind. I turned right into the village and stopped at the shop for milk and bread.

'Whose is the funeral that just passed?' I asked the woman behind the counter.

'Oh, that Cleary woman—you know the odd one with the bike from over by the lake? The brother found her dead in the bed the other day.'

*

She had lasted just one summer. The thought struck me that she might have had a premonition, a foreshadow of her own death, and opened her front door in early summer and ventured out to confirm that this place—such a place as this—had really existed, and she was not mad after all. Or only a little mad—just enough to discern some dark knowledge, a latent memory in her cells that sensed the stirrings of a new omen.

I went over there that evening, parked in the pub car park and walked along the road towards her house. Behind me I could hear the old Guinness sign swinging in the breeze. A bird flew low across my path, heading for the lake, its long scraggy neck almost level with my eyes. Then I was standing between the two pillars in front of her house, looking in. It was a long low bungalow with three small windows and a green door. I walked in the drive and around the back. Her bicycle was lying against the gable end of the house. A bag of turf sat outside the back door. I peered in the windows but could make out little through the dense net curtains. I tried the handle of the back door. A few fields away, a cow lowed. I sat on a low stone wall for a while. I did not like to think of her silence, like a dark mass enclosing her for years.

I was gazing at the window, squinting at the lacy pattern on the net curtains. Then something compelled me to rise and step forward. Something guided my hand to the base of the window frame. It slid up easily on its sash. I parted the curtains and raised my leg and bent my back and stepped into her bedroom. The light was dim. A clock ticked loudly. There was an unmade bed, a wardrobe, a dressing table, a private feeling. I walked through the house. In the kitchen there were newspapers strewn on the floor. Dirty dishes in the sink and half-filled jars and tins and packets of soup on the table. I wandered back to her bedroom and opened the wardrobe. The sickly smell of unwashed jumpers, old shoes. I turned around. I wanted something—a prayer book, a photograph, a diary maybe. I opened a drawer of the dressing table. Two pairs a diary maybe. I opened a drawer of the dressing table. Two pairs of dark socks that might have belonged to a man or a woman. Rosary beads. In the bottom drawer a medical textbook for nurses. I picked it up. From inside the back cover I lifted out a yellow page from an old newspaper, unfolded it and moved to the window for light.

It was pages three and four of the London *Evening Standard*, dated 22 November 1971. Six climbers dead in Scotland. Fighting in the Boyra peninsula in East Pakistan. The death of a famous footballer, aged forty-seven. Near the bottom of the page a court report. I began to read. The two defendants, aged nineteen and twenty-six, were convicted of robbery and aggravated sexual assault with intent of degradation on a 23-year-old Irish nurse in Dulwich. The victim was not named. They broke into her flat early one morning armed with a wheel brace and a hacksaw and subjected her to a terrifying ordeal lasting several hours. They cut off her nightdress and underwear with a Stanley knife, threatened to cut off her nipples unless she lay face down on the bed with her arms outstretched. With the Stanley knife they sliced her from neck to waist, slashed her buttocks, carved a vile word on her back. They sexually assaulted her with the wheel brace. Before they left they ransacked the flat and cut off the woman's hair.

In the dusk the corners of the room had disappeared. I stared at the unmade bed. I thought of an earthquake, a lateral shifting of the plates at her core. I pictured her waking in the mornings in that room, staring at the ceiling, then opening the window to a blue sky after night rain. And being caught for an instant, being taken down again by a memory, a dream, an aftershock. Don't tell me she didn't remember, don't tell me she didn't dream. And why did she not howl?

She was in her coffin a mile away. I thought of the tiny drop of time, the second—the fraction of a second—when the spark of an idea is ignited in a criminal mind. The second that explodes into being and begets an act that changes everything. That changed her, and flattened her out, and spread her so thinly that the space between parts of her, the space between her head and her heart, between all her nerve endings, grew so vast that she became almost entirely empty and in no time at all, in a morning, she disappeared.

And where was I that morning? Taking tea and toast with a novel propped, measuring out with exactitude a spoonful of sugar? Watching fog crawl over my back wall and tracking a thought with an intensity of being, as the blade pressed and pierced and punctured?

Suddenly she was standing at my aunt's door again, at my mercy. Would a nod have saved her, altered her fate? Or does fate defy alteration and play out as originally intended, a little later perhaps, a little differently? Would another calamity have lain in wait for her? For us? A tree crushing our car on a winter's night, crushing the two of us and our children? I think of these things now. I see possibilities everywhere—I see the thin veil that separates us from disaster. I see it shimmering above bodies of water, and loose slates; I see it in lightning flashes and speeding motorbikes; even in the rafters of my own attic, I see it lifting. And what good is Homer now? And where have all the gods gone—will Zeus climb down and help me? And, when the time comes, who will pay Charon?

Now I sit in the static of each day. I sit and wait for winter or for some hint of what to do next. I do not think of Suzanne as dead. I think of her in a dark room trying to recompose herself, rummaging for some remnant of memory, reaching out for an organ—an eye, a heart—and trying to fit it inside her. I dreamt of her the other night. I was walking along the road beyond by the lake. It was dusk and she was coming towards me again, her hair wild. As she drew near she looked at me and opened her mouth and began speaking in tongues.

THE ASTRAL PLANE

'I tried to give up God once,' she said.

It was morning and they were driving along the coast road at the edge of the Burren. On their left the Atlantic lay very still and beautiful and blue, and for a moment she found it almost impossible to think of it as merely sea.

Her husband looked straight ahead. 'You tried to give up God?'

'Yes, years ago. Before I met you.'

'And?' he said, turning briefly to look at her, 'How did that go?'

She looked out the window. He had a way of making her smile. 'Not very well, actually. He punished me—He took away my sleep.'

For as long as she could remember, she had pondered God. It wasn't so much fear of Him as gratitude for the particular life given, a good life, and a sense that at any moment, in her next breath, it might all end.

They were silent then and she was grateful. She had thought that a week away from the city would reveal some truths, some answers, and fix her thoughts more firmly. Outside the car the sun washed everything in its pale light, giving the stone walls, the lunar rocks, even the morning itself, a feeling of fragility.

Something came adrift in her that day. They drove to Spanish Point and sat on the rocks by the water. Adam took her hand and ran his fingers over hers. That evening they sat in the hotel lounge watching the other guests come and go—middle-aged Americans, young couples with children, businessmen down from the city for the golf at Lahinch. Outside, the light was fading. She got up and went to the window. Soon the moon would rise. There were rose bushes and fuchsias in the borders. There was no tree for miles around. Sometimes on their drives they came upon a lone bush on the roadside and she was stirred by its stark beauty, its forlornness.

Beyond the hotel garden the sea turned grey. She heard its murmur as the night began to fall. The nights here made her unspeakably lonely.

Adam got them drinks. There were lamps lighting in corners.

'I was thinking we might go back tomorrow,' she said.

He looked at her. 'Aren't you having a nice time? I thought we were having a nice time.'

'We are. It's lovely. It's just that, well… there's rain coming and we'd be going home on Saturday anyway. I just thought…' She knew the sky would soon turn purple and send down rain while they slept. In the morning she would gaze out of the hotel room onto grey rocks and she could not bear to think of the emptiness that would follow.

'Okay, if that's what you want.' He looked at her. 'Aren't you happy?'

He would always say the right words, do the right thing. He would put himself in harm's way for her. She should be happy. *She should be happy.* How then could she explain why she didn't feel enough? Is there a measure for enough? And when the enough plateaus out, as it does in a long marriage, is there a different kind of measure? Is there an index for love? She looked over at him, at his dark eyes and greying temples. And is there, she wondered, any explanation why on this warm night in this beautiful corner of the earth, with the vast ocean beyond the window and the moonlight overhead—is there any explanation why my head is filled with thoughts of another man?

They drove east to the city in near silence the next day. She had thought that faith, belief, would save her from this desolation, from the death of hope. That faith would protect against temptation, prevent this slide in life, make acceptable those mundane days when no more adventure, no new love, was possible again. Because love had, by now, been decided, accepted, finalised.

She had never met this other man, or heard his voice, and she had tried not to love him. On a wet evening in February she had attended an author's reading in the city. Afterwards, she had walked out into the lighted streets with the image of the soft-spoken writer and his novel with its strange aloof character swirling around in her head. Two weeks later she received an e-mail.

Hi there. Did you, by any chance, attend a reading in a Dublin library one evening last month? Did you leave your copy of Julius Winsome behind? I picked it up, and failing to find its owner among the stragglers, kept it. What a novel! I had not heard of this writer before. His book truly captivated me. I found this e-mail address inside the back cover. If this is your book I want to thank you and return it to you. If not, please accept my apologies for the intrusion. Sincerely,
E. B., New York.
P.S. I happened to be in Dublin for work when I strolled into the library that evening.

The memory of the reading returned—the hushed atmosphere, the author's stillness, the enclosed world of the novel.

Dear E, You have indeed correctly identified the owner of Julius. And yes, what a writer! You can hold onto the novel. And I hope you

*enjoyed your trip to this grimy old city of ours. And, lucky you,
living in NYC!*
Kind regards,
A. D.

Within five minutes her mailbox pinged.

Dear A,
*I sent that mail out into the ether never really expecting a reply. Just
shows you! And thanks for leaving Julius with me. I will read it
again—though I live in the shadow of a tower of unread books. And
alas, I do not reside in NYC but way out in the suburbs. Think*
Revolutionary Road *without the revolution, or the front lawn. Or
the beige.*
Best regards,
E

She sat looking at the words on the screen, and then went
downstairs to watch the evening news with Adam.

E,
*They're remaindering Julius here. I've bought three to give away at
Christmas. It will kill me to part with even one, but there you go.
And beige is very underrated.*

Dear A,
*A Christmas shopper in March, I'm impressed! And I loved Dublin
but I got robbed the night before I left. Think of it... a few Dublin
Jackeens getting the better of a tough Bronx boy. I felt so stupid.*
Regards,
E

She stared at the words, then shut down her laptop.

Dear A,
I wanted to ask if you had read any of Donovan's other books—I

*believe there are two? And my wife is a big fan of Irish writing—
what other contemporary writers can you recommend?*

And so it started. In his persistence she sensed a need. She
slipped in a reference to Adam the second night. It was all about
books and films and TV at the start. She had always had a need to
talk about books. He quoted Beckett and Sartre from memory. He
possessed an odd combination of bookish charm and boyish
hyperactivity. His glittering intelligence, in those first weeks,
terrified her. One day, she thought, my small seam of knowledge
will be exhausted. He peppered his opinions with quotes from
Swift and Goethe and she slipped further out of her depth. Sorry,
she replied, I have never read *Moral Purpose*. Sorry, I'm not very
well versed in German literature. Sorry, I'm not that up on
philosophy. Sorry, sorry, sorry. *Oh, I think you underestimate yourself,*
he wrote back. He sent her quotations, lines from songs; he sent her
poems. Did he not know the effect such words, such lines, such
poems might have on a woman?

*Your erudition leaves me tongue-tied. I'll soon need shades on this
side of the astral plane to shield me from the glare of your knowledge.*

His reply was slow in coming.

*The Astral Plane… I like this… Celestial beings, you and I… There
is a lonely spot near the South Pole—I read of this today—a US team
of astronomers are setting up an observatory there. It's the perfect site
for stargazing… I thought of you when I read this. It's so calm in this
place that there's almost no wind or weather there at all, and the sky
is dark and dry. It is the calmest place on earth. I thought of you.*

*I have so little to say, to write. What I write must seem very trite to
you.*

Why do you do this, why do you put yourself down like this?

*

He wrote copy for an advertising agency. He worked from a home office and made occasional trips to the city or abroad. She imagined a suburban town, like White Plains or Scarsdale and men in suits parking at the train station and boarding silver bullet trains that raced through the countryside, leaving telephone wires zinging in their wake, into the heart of Manhattan. He looked out on treetops from his upstairs office, he told her. He had a view of the sky and another of birds and birdhouses. He went down and counted the trees in his garden one day, for her. Eighteen, he said. Big garden, she said. He did not mention children. He told her there were woodlands at the back and cardinals in the trees. She did not know what cardinals looked like so she lifted down Adam's bird book from the bookcase. She began to imagine it all. She gave him the sound of running water close by and a lake a mile away and the silver train in the distance, and starlings wheeling in formation above his head, and she gave him a wide open sky as he crossed the fields, and a yellow sun, and a ready open heart.

There is this girl I meet. She works in my local mini-market. One day she was sitting on the wall in the parking lot, crying. She's just a kid, eighteen or nineteen. She's from a farm in Mississippi and her husband's stationed up here with the army. She calls me 'Mister'. The others bully her over her accent. She's poor. I can tell the poor. I grew up poor, I married a poor girl. The poor have a code: they stay together, loyal, faithful too. She's missing her mother, this girl. The poor always get to you.

I dreamt of you last night. I woke before dawn and heard your footsteps on the stairs. I felt you drawing near and I was frightened you'd be discovered. The moonlight streamed in through the skylight on the landing. I walked barefoot through the house. I knew you were just ahead of me. I opened the back door and there in the middle of the garden stood a deer. The moon was so bright. He stood and looked into my eyes with his own beautiful wet ones, and then he turned and I saw there was a stream at the end of the garden and, beyond that, a dark forest. He bounded off and disappeared into the forest. I fled upstairs and each step of the stairs fell away behind me.

One evening Adam came in and placed a kiss on her forehead and rubbed her back and then walked out onto the patio.

'Will we eat out here?' he called.

He helped her carry out the plates and glasses. Her hands trembled. Earlier, on the canal bridge, she had driven through a red light.

'I ran into Kevin in town today,' he said, when they were seated. 'He looked a wreck.'

'Things aren't great at home,' she said. 'I told you.'

'Yeah, I know. But it's just the usual stuff with them, right?'

She shrugged. 'Karen doesn't think so. She wants out.'

'She wants out? Why? What's he done?'

'Nothing. He hasn't done anything. It's—I don't know… They're incompatible, she says.'

'Incompatible! Huh! New-fashioned love!'

She gave him a look.

'What? It's true, isn't it? *Incompatible.* Christ, you'd think people were software programmes—"X is incompatible with your system, sir! You'll need a whole new system, or, alternatively, you may change X."'

'It's not funny.'

'I know… Sorry… There's no third party, is there? Jesus, has he met someone else?'

'No. No. I don't think so.'

'And he's not drinking or… violent, is he? Or gambling?'

'No, no, nothing like that.' She put on her sunglasses and looked at the sky. She longed to escape his presence.

'What then? They've just grown tired of each other, is that it?'

She shrugged. 'I don't know. I suppose so.' Suddenly she hated the sky. She wanted no reminder of blue or beauty or betrayal. She went inside and lifted a jug of water from the fridge and leaned on the door for a few moments.

'That's what people do now, isn't it?' he said. 'They break up so easily.' His voice had grown sad.

'People don't break up easily. They don't.' He seemed not to hear her.

'No one is satisfied anymore. Everyone wants more. We all think we're special, but we're not.'

'They've fallen out of love,' she said, a little harshly.

She felt his eyes on her. After a few moments she pushed her chair back and got up.

'You okay?'

She frowned and shrugged. 'Of course.'

That night she lay in the bath and wept. She heard Adam move about downstairs. She had done him harm. As she had done the woman, the astral wife, harm. Each night that she ascended the stairs and sat at her desk she was stealing from his life, from his wife. Is this what she had become—a thief, a plunderer? She heard the signature tune of the ten o'clock news. She went into the bedroom and lay on the bed. This day, and every day, and her whole conscious life now, started and ended with the other man, with the yearning for him. Was she allowed to yearn like this? Was it permitted? She heard Adam's step on the stairs. A tear rolled from the corner of her eye. He knelt at her side.

'Hey... Shh, what's wrong?' He took her hand and kissed it, and at his touch the guilt flared up inside her. 'Sometimes, I think... something isn't here anymore,' he whispered. 'Something's been taken. It frightens me.' Then he kissed her eyelids. 'What is it? What's wrong?'

She shook her head and smiled. 'Nothing, honest.' Then he rose and turned to go. He bent down and took her bare feet in his hands and kissed them. 'See?' he said brightly. 'See how much I love you?'

Things shifted on the plane then. She became hyper alert to every change in tone, every late mail or small absence. She thought he removed himself sometimes. She could not bear to think of him as a husband, as deeply married. She feared running out of things to say and strove to draw out the intimacy. But the effort showed. She became moody, began to pick and prod. She accused him of remoteness.

Me, remote? he countered in a blaze of anger that shocked her. Her curtness sometimes, he wrote, pierced him to the bone, and she was frosty, like so many European women. *Cold Northern Women,* he wrote in cruel capitals. *You're ice-bucket cold sometimes. And you have a sharpness that can pierce. Do you know this? Are you even aware of this?*

When was I cold? When did I pierce you? she demanded, in a tumble of rage and hurt and fear. *I have never said such cruel things to you, never once... And I am tired of this... this affair of the mind. And don't think it's less! That the damage and the betrayal and the guilt is less than the other? Is that what you think? Because it's not, it's worse. Do you think we'll go untouched, unpunished, you and I? Do you think we are immune? Do you? Is that what you think? And where's your code now?*

A rift opened, and their quarrel turned into a battle which left her profoundly shaken. Back and forth they traded hurts, damage heaped on damage. The astral plane fell silent for days. Each nightfall she became overwrought. His loss impoverished her. In the mornings she looked out at the trees and found a new calm. She got a taste of how it would feel to be clear of him. He had become an interruption in her life, a vexation. She would always be waiting for signs of the end, of him casting about for a new love. She would shed him and it would be an ease. Come the winter he would have faded out, and she would survive, she would endure. People don't die of love anymore, she thought. She could not die of love for a man she had never met. Could she?

Please, please come back to me... Are you not glad that I found you?

She read his plea at dawn. She crept back to bed. Adam lay on his belly and from the borders of sleep he reached out and drew her to him and whispered the familiar words and declarations he'd whispered every morning for years.

She climbed out of bed again and sat before the screen. She typed a word. *Refound.* She closed her eyes. She knew there would be nothing worse than losing him.

And so, somehow, a difficult passage had been managed. She walked around the house and out into the streets again, in glorious bounty, thinking, *I am loved, I am the beloved.* She felt his approach in unexpected moments: brushing off Adam in the kitchen, driving through the city at night, walking by the seashore. She had a longing to use ampler words, *my love, my darling.* At the water's edge she stood and waited, longing to detect something of him, some return, a sign, an echo carried back in the hum of the universe.

It might have continued like this, this strange courtly kind of love. Or the talk and the dreams might have petered out and given way to a new tranquility. And the desire, too, in time might have burned itself out for want of consummation. But then he hurled a lightning bolt down onto her screen one night.

I have to come to Dublin again. I didn't know if I should tell you. Then I thought... We might pass each other in the street; I might walk by a café with you inside the window, oblivious, like in Doctor Zhivago... *And I thought what a great tragedy that would be. But I don't know what to say now... except: Do you want to meet?*

She rode the commuter train into the city on a bright morning in mid-August. Small suburban back gardens shot past. Across from her a youth with a pale feminine face listened to his iPod, his long legs crossed and hidden under him so that she imagined him ending in a mermaid's tail.

She saw him first, standing directly under Bewley's clock. He wore a black jacket and his bag was slung over his shoulder, like he said it would be. She came down the street from Stephen's Green and he turned and the sun came out and fell on his face and she saw it was the astral man. He put his arms out and embraced her. She felt herself stiffen and shy at his touch. She could not look at him. She glanced around the street, thinking that Adam was watching.

'It's so good to see you. You look lovely. I'm so happy you came... I was so afraid you'd get cold feet...' His accent was strange in this place. 'How are you? Are you okay?... Please, say something...' He stood back from her.

She felt his eyes scorch her, from head to toe. 'How was the flight?'

'Good. Good. I like night flying. I got a couple of hours' sleep on the plane. But tell me... how are you? This is strange, isn't it? This is really strange... but nice too. Isn't this nice? What will we do? Would you like to get coffee or lunch or something? Do you want to sit down? I do! I need to sit down. Are you glad you came? Are you glad we're here?'

Stop talking, she longed to say. *Why can't you stop talking*?

They started up the street. She thought walking would quell him. A boy on roller skates came weaving towards them. He swerved close and she moved aside and bumped lightly against the astral man's shoulder. He placed a hand on her back and muttered 'Lunatic!' after the boy. She smiled at the word, and he gasped 'Aha!' His delight was contagious and she felt herself blush. 'I thought I'd lost you there for a while,' he said. 'You looked scared, as if I might be about to shoot you or something.'

All the time she felt his hand on her back.

He stopped and turned to her and touched the ends of her hair. He brought his forehead close to hers. He was whispering something but the racket inside her head and on the street drowned out his words. She pulled away and walked on.

'Please, aren't you going to talk to me? I've come all this way…'

'I thought you came for work.'

'Work came second. I came for you.'

They entered the Green and walked under the trees. Men in suits crossed the park on their lunch breaks. Teenagers, joggers, mothers with buggies went hurriedly by. She scanned each passing face. They sat on a bench, side by side, almost touching. A pigeon hopped on the path at their feet, pecking crumbs. The sun dipped behind a cloud. He put a hand on hers. She closed her eyes at the touch.

'I cannot stay long,' she said impassively.

He withdrew his hand. His jaw clenched, a muscle rippled. Her heart was pounding. If she touched him, if she as much as put a hand on his, there would be no going back.

'All morning I walked these streets,' he said, 'counting the minutes until you came.'

'I dreamt of you again last night,' she said. She tried to look at him and smiled. 'I have to stop dreaming of you.' His gaze settled on her. She let herself look into his eyes and for a few seconds felt herself incline towards him, like she was falling into him. She turned her head then and looked to the pond where ducks were gliding by. On the far side a small boy held out bread. 'I dreamt I had come to meet you, like this, now… But we were on a country road. Your hair was wet, as if you'd swum to me. You were looking around for shelter but the trees were bare and the sky was grey and you could not speak... The world was empty except for us. It wasn't real.'

He took her hands in his. She made two small tight fists. Slowly, finger by finger, he opened them. 'I'm real,' he said softly. 'I *can* speak.' His eyes held hers, imploring her.

The ducks flocked close to the boy.

'I've come all this way. Talk to me... please.'

'I don't know what to say. I'm afraid.'

He lifted her hand and kissed it. 'I wake in the night and it's you I see,' he whispered.

She was afraid he would say more than she could bear. She looked away. Must we succumb to every desire, she thought, every appetite? A siren screeched from the north of the Green and startled her. And isn't the sin in the thought, in the intention, as much as in the act? His eyes were searching her, searing into her, seeing everything. As if he were peeling back her skin, exposing every nerve, reading every nerve's story.

The siren grew louder. She thought it was coming for her—the ambulance, the police were coming for her. 'Tell me,' he pleaded through the siren's whine, 'tell me what you want.'

'I want my hand back,' she said.

Immediately she regretted the hurt but did not know how to undo it. She needed his mercy then. They looked at each other. She saw what was inside him, his sorrow, his terrible striving. He was striving for something more than her—for the crux of something. He was straining for some centre, some source, something in himself that he was trying to decode. She felt his enormous struggle. She would have liked to lead him to it, and place it back inside him.

'I brought you a present,' he said softly and placed a small blue package in her hand.

'What is it? Thank you. I didn't...'

'Don't open it now.'

He buried his hands in his pockets and looked straight ahead. She leaned in and kissed his cheek. He hung his head, overcome. She moved close, against him, touching the side of his body. They sat completely still. Then he leaned forward, and put his head in his hands. She sensed his withdrawal, felt it as an immense loss. She knew he was moving away, scoping out from her. A new fear began to creep into her. Slowly his conjugal life rose into view. The ordinary days with a wife, children maybe; the nights, sweet and imperfect. The pain that binds people. In those moments she felt the scales tipping. She thought it was all catching up with him here, now, and that he had come to the brink. Suddenly she knew he could not violate that life; he could not inflict that wound. It would mark his heart. She looked up at the trees and watched a leaf fall to the ground at their feet. She could not bear the thought of his sorrow. She could not bear the guilt of his guilt.

'I have to go now,' she said.

He turned to her. 'Please, please don't go.' With each word his voice seemed to ebb away. She had an image of him being lifted and placed in her arms, draped over her and she holding him, bearing his weight.

She fled the city on foot. Traffic lights and hard shiny surfaces rose to meet her and the sky pressed down on her. She reached the canal as the first drops of rain began to fall. She floated under trees. She was moving further and further out of his orbit and soon he would no longer detect her.

She rushed headlong into her kitchen and opened cupboard doors and ran water and peeled potatoes. The kitchen sounds penetrated her with their tedious comforting familiarity. She sat down with Adam and they ate in silence. She watched the summer rain fall outside.

Then she climbed the stairs. On the landing she touched her face in the mirror. She sat at her desk and opened his blue box. She lifted out a small silver bracelet with a turquoise stone at its centre and rubbed the stone between her finger and thumb. She saw her reflection in the window. She would never find a word for his loss.

She sat looking out, listening to the rain, for a long time. It would prevail, this astral presence, beyond tonight and tomorrow, beyond next week and next year. Her heart had been recast. What had happened could not be put back. She would endure it.

She switched on her laptop. She would trawl back through his mails now, feel his old words clutch at her one last time, before deletion. She signed in and waited. He was out there in the city, across rooftops, listening to the rain too. The Inbox appeared and there came, simultaneously, the delicate ping that announced new mail and she sat up and the ping lingered—so minute and pure and beautiful tonight, as if a new note had been struck and added to the scale, a tiny secret sign issuing from him, a newfound sound. Her hand trembled on the mouse. She opened his mail, read his newly minted words and felt herself capsize. She closed her eyes. She knew she could not be without him. She remembered his shoulder touching hers, his imploring eyes, and she felt herself again in his gaze—poised, silent, immaterial—and she knew she would die a thousand times at this memory, at this confluence of hearts. She leaned towards the screen and thought it was not an endurance at all, this presence, this plane, and as the night came down and the rain fell on the city it came to her that what this was—this man, this moment—what this was, most of all, was the resurrection of hope.

LITTLE DISTURBANCES

He hears music when he wakes these mornings. The notes float up from below, pouring softly into the room, and for a moment he thinks it is Miriam, Miriam perched on the piano stool with her legs swinging and the purple-flowered wallpaper swirling around her and the notes spilling from her fingers. He has started to expect it when he opens his eyes each morning and finds the patch of sky out the window. He says nothing to Marie because, of course, there is no music, the music is in his head and Miriam is in Canada, a grown woman living alone in a beautiful glass house set into a wooded hill above Vancouver. When she looks out her windows she can see the Pacific Ocean. In winter her fingers used to break out with eczema. Once, she ran to the end of the yard to call him in for his tea. He was leaning on a gate looking out over the fields. *Why are the hills blue, Daddy?* Her eyes squinted at the hills in the distance. Because they're far away, he said. *What's behind them?* More hills. *I want to see over them.* He lifted her up on a rung of the gate. *Higher, Daddy.* The sun was warm on their faces. *Why are you crying, Daddy?* He had an urge to take her hand and start walking towards the distant hills. They would rest under the shade of lone trees and then walk on in silence, forever. He wonders if her hands still break out now in the cold of Canada or if she keeps a piano in the glass house.

'Will you eat a boiled egg?' Marie asks when he comes into the kitchen. 'For a change?'

He crosses the tiled floor and steps into the sunlight. He has a small flash of last night's dream. 'I don't think so,' he says. 'Just the toast'll be grand.'

She lifts the teapot from the range. She spreads butter and marmalade, thickly, on a slice of toast, and leaves it on his plate. The sun falls on the pot of marmalade, on the chunky orange peel inside the glass, and his mouth waters. A white cat jumps up on the windowsill outside and hunkers down next to a black kitten. The nine o'clock news comes on the radio and the cat begins to wash.

'Finish the slice of toast,' she says and looks him in the eye. 'Are you not hungry?'

He lifts the toast and bites and chews it slowly. He adds a spoon of sugar to his tea.

'The surgery rang,' she says. 'Kathy said they have the results back. You're to go up at 12 and he'll see you.'

He looks at her. She had her hair done yesterday. Her eyes are a watery blue, almost grey, behind her glasses.

'Do you remember what Miriam used to call us?' he asks.

She lifts her cup and looks at him.

'She used to call us swans,' he says.

'Did you not hear what I said? Kathy said you're to go up and see Dr O'Byrne.' She puts the cup down and looks away.

They were all there at the dinner table one Sunday after James's wedding, fifteen years ago, and the talk turned to marriage and Miriam came out with it: *There aren't many swans left anymore. Like Mam and Dad… mating for life.* When he was a young man he stood in the turlough field one evening watching the swans that came to winter on his lough. They were hard and brutish. He remembered a story from national school, the Children of Lir, three brothers and a sister who were turned into swans for five hundred years. The swans in his school book were lovely creatures. He stood back from the water that evening, from the swallow holes that could suck an animal underground and drag it through channels that flowed down from the bog. He was afraid of the pull of water. There was something in him and he thought the water knew it. The swans rose that evening and passed over his head. He turned around and saw a lone tree, and its bare branches against the sky nearly broke him.

'You might do that run yourself,' he says.

'Sure we can go together.'

'It's a wonder she didn't tell you the results over the phone.'

'They never do that. The doctor has to see you himself.'

'There must be something wrong,' he says. 'They'd tell you if there wasn't.'

'Ah, no, not necessarily. It might be something small, some small irregularity… like that thyroid problem Pádraig had… Do you remember—he was feeling terrible for months before they got to the bottom of it?'

'It's not some small irregularity.'

The clock ticks on the wall behind her. He never forgets that she is here. She looks out the window. She has a way of being distant that makes him think he is already invisible. One day at the dinner she turned to him and said 'Can you not chew any quieter?' In winter her eyes are bluer—he used think the cold got in. A frown gathers on her brow now. Once, he knew all that went on behind that brow. Once she had been as delicate as a sparrow in his hands. He had called her *My little one* and almost died with the need to be near her.

The sickness has been inside him for months. In early spring he walked through the land, going deeper into the fields to the last hill. He moved up the slope and stood on the summit and was caught suddenly by the ground shifting. He began to list as if on a ship. He turned his head and saw the dark mouths of foxes' dens along the ditch. Once, when he was baling hay late on a summer's evening he saw a vixen approach her den. A clutch of young cubs peeped out, anxious, and at the sight of the mother, came scrambling over each other, not orphaned after all. He imagined them all moving underneath him now, loosening the earth, tumbling through dark tunnels—a teeming world of foxes inside the hill. In winter they'd sleep, curled in a tight circle. The hill began to pitch that day and the sky spun. The bile rose up and he retched onto the summit. He longed for the cover of trees then, to stand under the beech tree and feel rain falling on the leaves. He thought of small birds sheltering under their canopy and when the rain stopped, the sound of rainwater trickling down pipes.

Marie is standing in the middle of the kitchen looking up. 'Those damn flies,' she says. The flies circle around the light fitting. She goes to the cupboard and brings out a spray can. She comes at them and aims, and they dart about drunkenly in the poison mist.

'Wouldn't it be an ease if we had it all behind us?' he says. He means dying. He knew a man once who took his own life. He parked his car at the crossroads on Christmas Eve and switched off the engine and blew his head off with a shot gun. He had left his wife and four kids at the church for Midnight Mass. Marie and himself were at Midnight Mass the same night.

The black kitten jumps off the windowsill. 'Stop that talk,' she says and goes to the back door.

On a summer's evening when he was thirty he had found her. He had walked across a wooden dance floor under a tarpaulin marquee and stood before her, as if she had sent out a call to him. She said she liked his name, that it was a mild name and he must be a mild man. But then she went to America. Six months later, out of the blue, she returned and married him and delivered him headlong into the world of woman. Every night her creamy skin, her whispers, silenced him. In the distance he would hear the bleating of a lamb or the call of a bird at dawn. She would sit up and take an infant to her and nurse him. She would whisper to him to pass her nightie or some other womanly item, and though he had recently inherited a house and a farm and a herd of cattle they were nothing compared with these whispers. *Only you and I know these nights*, he thought. She came out to the fields in daytime and said *I want to stay here with you*, the way a child would say it. He did not want her to lift a finger—to turn a sod of turf or raise a sheaf of corn. *Leave that alone*, he told her, as she tossed hay from a fork, her face red and beaded with sweat. *Leave that alone and go in and bring us out a drink*. When they stopped to rest she took off his shoes and socks. *Stop that*, he said, and laughed. The sun beat down on her arms. She stretched out her legs and pressed her bare feet to his. She closed her eyes and whispered *I'm happy now*, and he thought she drifted off for a minute.

He moves to the armchair and she clears away the breakfast things. He is watching her feet on the tiles. When James and the girls stand beside her he is amazed that this grown man and these grown women came out of such a small woman. James comes in at night with news of the day, the work, the grandchildren. Sally and Sheila come down from Dublin every few weekends, sometimes bringing their husbands and children. They bring wine too and lay it on a shelf in the fridge and late on a Friday night they pour Marie a glass. He is not a drinker and when he settles in to watch the news and the *Late Late Show* they carry the bottle and the glasses over to the dining room and he hears the hum of their talk and occasional laughing. Marie has gone from him little by little, year after year, and the going is almost complete. He has never been enough; she had wanted a fuller life, and a small bit of glamour. The years wore her down, the worry, the work. In the early days he used to think she regretted returning from America. They went to a dinner dance at Christmas once and she wore a black maxi dress with a white trim at the neck. After the meal he spun her round the dance floor too hard, too fast, to make her remember him. On winter nights with the whole house asleep he would come on a film. It was always America, with handsome men in suits, Gregory Peck and Cary Grant and James Stuart, and beautiful still women, Grace Kelly and Deborah Kerr, and his heart would swell at the talk and the look of the lovers. At the end he'd sit back and realise that what he felt too was the terrible sickness of love.

Something spills out of us, he thinks, and it cannot be put back again. Out of nowhere he thinks of Miriam in her glass house above the ocean.

'D'you remember when Miriam used to have those fainting spells?' Marie asks, turning to him. 'When she used to black out for five or ten minutes?'

He has no words. He looks at her. They have remembered Miriam at the same moment and he feels a surprising wave of hope. 'You have to remember it,' she pleads. 'I used to run out to the fields to you in an awful state, carrying her in my arms. She was six or seven at the time. D'you not remember?'

He stares at her. She has been doing this lately, pulling up old memories that rattle him.

'It was frightening,' she says. 'It happened when she got upset... She'd cry and cry and get worked up into a terrible state... and her eyes would roll back in her head... And then she'd just fall off unconscious.'

He was up on the tractor and mower in the middle of a meadow one day when she came running out with the child in her arms, the head flopping as she ran. He jumped down and took her and laid her on the ground. He thought the stubble on her bare arms and legs would prod her back to life.

'Do you think we neglected her?' Marie asks suddenly.

'No, no, we did not. Didn't you bring her to the doctor?'

She nods. 'He had some name for it—some emotional condition—he said she'd grow out of it, and she did, after a year or two.'

They were kneeling over her that day. Her eyelids moved and when she opened her eyes she had a terrible look. He thought she must have seen things she couldn't bear. She whispered *Daddy*.

The radio is on low and the presenter is reading out the local death notices.

'"Scarlet Ribbons",' he says, half to himself.

She looks over at him.

'That's what she used to play on the piano, "Scarlet Ribbons",' he says. 'She learned it off that Jim Reeves record.'

But Marie is gazing out the window. 'She was always very impressionable. I was always afraid of who she might fall in with. I don't know where she got it… all that fainting, all that feeling.'

On Sundays in August Marie would dress the girls in little summer dresses and pack a picnic and they'd all drive to Salthill. She'd get a faraway look in her eyes when the sea came into view. He thought she was remembering some American place—Coney Island, maybe. One weekend they went to his brother's holiday caravan in Lahinch. The kids played all day and got sunburnt and she cooked a big dinner in the evening and they ate outside with the sun going down. While she was putting the kids to bed he walked over the dunes and stood looking at the sea. Dusk started to fall. Then she was beside him. They said nothing but walked along the water's edge. They sat on the hard sand with the little waves almost touching them, then moving further and further out. After a long time they got up and walked back. The dark was coming down around their heads. When they got to the door of the caravan he thought they were different, a different man and woman. That night he had a dream that he was sinking into the sea and she was in a small boat with the moon above her head. He was crying out to her and her eyes were wet with tears but she could not put a hand out to him. The following winter he found her in the cow house one night, sitting on the steps, smoking, with the rain tapping on the galvanised roof and the cows stirring in the stalls around her. 'What's wrong with you?' he said.

Maybe they should have gone to America. Maybe they would have been different people in America. He would not have lingered in fields on summer evenings or stood alone in the shed on winter nights, putting off going inside. He had put it to her once, before the wedding.

'My uncle Johnny is in San Francisco,' he said. 'He sent word that one of us lads should go out to him and he'll sponsor us. He works in the fire department. There'd be a good wage.'

She thought about it and then frowned. 'They get earthquakes in California. I'd be afraid. My aunt Molly told me.'

He had never heard that. 'I don't know,' he said. 'I don't think they're dangerous.'

She looked out of the car window where they were sitting after a dance. 'It would be like eloping. It wouldn't look good.'

In the mid-morning Marie calls the surgery and then drives to town to keep the appointment. He walks to the front of the house and down the steps under the arched trellis with the pink roses. There are flowerpots on the windowsills, overflowing with pink and white flowers. He stands and looks at them. Lately, a strangeness has come on him. He sees and hears things that were once beyond him—the buzz of insects, the humming of electric cables, the blood drumming through his head. He gets flashes too—like the foxes under the hill—and one night he had a vision of all the animals he ever reared and sent off for slaughter, all standing before him on an open plain, looking into his eyes. He never tells Marie these things. He would like to, but he is afraid that it is too late. He wishes he had done something for her, some gesture, one big thing. Built her a house, maybe. Or planted an orchard. Or said something, one glorious thing—that her eyes remind him of a wolf's and he loves wolves because they're wild and lonesome, or that he is afraid for her all the time now, and himself too, and he cannot bear it when she leaves his side.

At the front gate he sees Christy Kelly, bucket in hand, crossing the road towards his yard.

'You're late milking her,' he calls out, moving towards Christy.

'Ah, I am, I am. Sure it's only a hobby at this stage. No one inside there'll touch a drop of it, when it's not pasteurised.'

'No. We didn't have it pasteurised years ago and we did all right.' The white cat comes down the steps and brushes against his legs. He bends down and strokes her. 'I suppose you can always give it to the cats.' The cat rolls on her back, exposing herself. He thinks of the little organs inside her belly.

'Christ, no. I can't abide cats.'

'And what do you do with the milk so—when you have no calves to feed?'

'I fuck it down the drain.'

He looks up at the sky. In the distance he hears a sheep bleat and all at once he is seized by its sound and last night's dream returns to him. He is sick in a hospital bed, late at night. The door opens slowly and a little procession of lambs enters and his heart leaps and he is amazed and overjoyed at this miracle, and as he raises himself on his elbow the drip comes loose. The little procession marches to the edge of his bed and the first lamb is about to speak. He looks into the lamb's eyes and starts to cry. Then Miriam is standing in the doorway, smiling because she has brought all the lambs to visit him, as if they are her children. She is holding a sickly newborn in her arms. She leaves it on the bed beside him, and goes to fix the tubes and when he looks up he sees that it is a nurse, and not Miriam, who has come to fix things. 'I'll just pop this back in again… ' she says and with a little flick of her wrist, she inserts the needle into the newborn lamb's leg.

'Marie feeds a few cats in there every morning,' he says to Christy when he recovers himself. He gives a little nod in the direction of the white cat at his feet. 'I think they're company for her.'

'Christ, she'll only be drawing them around the place doing that,' Christy says. 'They'll breed like anything.' He waves his arm to hunt the cat away. 'The bloody things are a nuisance. I came out from milking the cow a couple of mornings ago and left the bucket on the wall for a minute to wash my hands and when I turned around hadn't one of them his big head within in it, drinking it? Well, if I had the gun handy I'd have shot the bastard… And that was the second or third time that happened. They're filthy, you know, they carry every disease known to man.'

'They keep the rats away at least.'

'Ah, they do and they don't.'

He walks around the back, the day stretching ahead. He wants something to happen but is afraid of what it might be. At the end of the yard he rests his arms on the top rung of the gate. He fills his pipe with tobacco and lights it and gazes at the cattle and the hills in the distance. They have not seen Miriam in five years. She's afraid to fly now. He pictures her in Vancouver, with her friends. He draws deeply on his pipe and then bites on the stem and becomes agitated. When she was eighteen they had a falling out. He did not like the lad she was going around with during her first summer home from college. The lad's father was a drunk and he knew enough about men and human nature to know that the lad, no matter how decent he was in his youth, would turn out like the father. When she skipped down the steps on a summer's evening and got into the lad's car and drove off, he couldn't bear it. He lay awake at night waiting for her key in the door, demented. Marie said to let it go, that it might fizzle out in time. But then, on a night out in a town not far away, he came face to face with the father's drunken leer. *Who's the big shot now*? And then he laughed. *Isn't she the lovely girleen! We might be related yet, Mick.*

The next weekend with her gone off in the lad's car again, the words boiled up in his brain, the leer, the glass in his hand as he swayed, the coat with the dirty sleeves. In the early hours the front door opened and he jumped out of bed and pounded along the landing and down the stairs. He raised his hand but could not bring it down on her, so he brought his fist down on the kitchen table instead. He was not to darken the door again, he roared. She turned white but he could not stop his pacing, his raging.

The lad was never mentioned again. She returned, still, at weekends and in the summer—a quieter girl, he thought, because everything has a price. After university she got a job in a city library, and then a few years later she went to Canada.

The quiet of the day is blown apart by a terrible bang, and he is startled. A flock of starlings rises out of the trees. He walks down the road towards Kelly's yard, tracking the sound that's still rolling in waves through the air. He meets Christy walking out of his yard. He is carrying a gun and raises it in salute.

'Christy, are you all right?'

'Never better.'

'I thought I heard a shot.'

'The fuckin' cat knocked over the bucket of milk this time.' He nods in satisfaction and walks on. 'He won't do it again, the bastard.'

He crosses Kelly's yard, past the dairy and the open barn door. In the furthest corner the bucket is lying on its side in a pool of milk. Blobs of dirt float on its surface. He feels a chill on the back of his neck. He looks over the wall into the field. The cat's corpse is lying on the grass five or six yards away. The head is flattened, the belly open with little twisted ropes of intestines and fur and blood. Flies are starting to swarm. He feels his legs grow weak, and the force of the bullet in his own middle. He moves his gaze to the paws, all four, tender, white. He closes his eyes for a second, lifts his face to the sun, as the bile begins to rise.

He is sitting on the low wall at the edge of the front lawn, waiting. A white butterfly lands on a flower. He had never noticed butterflies or flowers much before. His shoulders are tired. Out on the main road a heavy truck goes by. He tracks the sound of its engine as it passes the shop, the church, the graveyard. The sky darkens. A cloud gathers directly above him, and seems to hang there for a minute. It starts to mushroom out then. He has the feeling that it will lower itself down over him. His heart thumps faster. He feels some danger close by, as if the cloud has come to pester him or question him, and when he has no answers, it will press down on him and enclose him and smother him. He closes his eyes tight and then, for no reason, he turns his head and there among Marie's red dahlias is the white butterfly. He watches its wings moving. He feels a little release, as if the cloud is lifting. For a second he is free. He feels some goodness, and that it is coming from the butterfly. He watches it flitting among the flowers. Then his breath catches and he thinks how something of Marie always revives him. He feels himself break. He should have talked to her more. He should have gone inside at night. He should have tried to coax her to California. He thinks of all the blindness he ever had.

Out on the main road, he hears the familiar sound of the Toyota slowing down. He sits up and waits for the engine to draw nearer, until he sees her head inside the car. She slows at the front gate. A look passes between them. A little piece of him, a lump of flesh or an organ, seems to break off inside and drift away. She drives into the car shed and switches off the ignition.

*

Soon she will lead him inside and in the kitchen she will tell him what he already knows. All day long they will move about the house with their separate thoughts. When the light fades they will sit in their chairs by the range. She will prompt him to retell a story from the past, and when he frowns and pauses halfway through she will reach down into his memory and pluck out the name or the date he has forgotten, and they will laugh and almost forget themselves. He will no longer be afraid to say things. When night comes they will lie down and he will tell her that she has never changed and that her blue-grey eyes remind him of a wolf's. He will tell her that there was always some want in him and he is afraid of almost everything now. He will ask her to send for Miriam. He will remind her that the front of the graveyard gets waterlogged in winter, and to go well back towards the end. *Pick a dry grave for me*, he will say. *Don't bury me in water*.

ROOM IN HER HEAD

Romy watched the Americans go down the lane. Bob carried the fishing rods and Susan walked beside him. She wore a yellow T-shirt and sunglasses in her hair. At the end of the lane they turned right onto the road in the direction of the lake, nearly a mile away. Romy looked at the mountains across the way. Just then a cloud covered the sun and shadows darkened the slopes. She saw the tiny figures of sheep grazing on slanted fields and imagined the sound of their faint plucking on the short grass. In winter the cold silver river sliced through the valley and the bare trees were silhouetted against the sky. She liked the stark beauty of winter. She thought about Bob and Susan for a while. Their absence left her feeling momentarily free.

She stood at the door and squinted into the dark interior. Michael was working on his laptop at the desk with his briefcase on the floor beside him. She wanted to speak, but something in the purposeful arrangement of his body deterred her. She brought a kitchen chair outside and sat against the white cottage wall and began to read.

Little things disturbed her; the strong sunlight on the page, children's laughter on the next farm, the ticking of a baler nearby. A blackbird on a branch of the ash tree opened its beak in song. At times all the sounds gathered and melded into one. The sun burned the top of her head and when she touched her hair she thought the hot brittle strands might ignite, and her whole head catch fire. Her novel was set in a frozen northern landscape and the main character an intense silent man who loved his neighbour's wife. Gradually she forgot herself and was drawn down into the book, into the man's suffering, into the cold white place, until suddenly it struck again—the gathering, the concordant notes of the baler and the cries of children and birds—and she closed her eyes and she was neither in the frozen north nor in the man's heart nor there burning up in the sun. She dropped her hand and touched the edge of the chair, relieved that it still contained her.

The cottage belonged to their American friends. Susan was an artist and professor in a university in the Midwest and Bob was a photojournalist. Romy had met Susan in a Dublin library a few years earlier, when Susan was experiencing a 'creative crisis'. The American woman had hoped that an intense shift to literature, to the deliberateness of words and language, might help unleash the internal visual images that had backed up in her psyche. She believed the rhythm of words, of poetry especially, would release her, free her of her affliction. This was how Susan spoke. She was ten years older than Romy. Bob was her third husband. She told Romy that she had proposed to him three weeks after they met.

'I popped the question and he looked at me for a moment and then he said, "Oh, I don't think so, babe… I'd make a bad husband." "That's ok," I told him, "I quite like bad husbands… I've had two. They amuse me."'

Romy had stared at Susan, taking a moment too long to register the words.

'Rosemary, honey, I'm *kidding*! That's a line!'

Bob was more boy than man, at times sluggish, other times volatile. He had fine Germanic features and blue eyes and straight blond hair. On their first trip to Ireland they found the cottage in the northwest and returned each summer. They converted the outhouses into a studio with white walls and a wooden floor and skylights in the roof. Every morning Susan donned an old shirt, and stood at her easel with her brushes and paint and her music swirling around her, composing and painting the large canvasses that shocked Romy with their derelict beauty. Limestone walls, ancient stone circles, blue-grey mountains and white suns, haunting portals and archways and always some mysterious figure at the edge—human or animal or bird—a lurking presence that made something flip over inside Romy and render her silent.

The afternoon was warm and still. She moved towards Michael and away from him, repeatedly. She feared the return of the Americans but did not know why. She made coffee and placed a mug at his elbow and then walked to the window.

'I think I'll go back to work,' she said.

He twisted his body towards her. 'You're joking.'

'No, I'm serious.'

They looked at each other. 'I knew this would happen,' he said.

'I have too much time. I don't need all this time.'

'You did before. You wanted time. That's what you wanted, you said.'

'That was then.'

She had thought she would recreate the long mornings of her youth spent in libraries. She thought she might recover something in the poems and novels from those years and take it back out with her, take it home to Michael, to both of them. But the words did not affect her in the way they once had, as if, in the intervening years, she had shed some of her imagination, or access was denied, or there was not enough room in her head for such words any more.

He turned back to his laptop, lifted the briefcase from the floor and removed some files. She looked out the window. She could not tell him that she was afraid. Lately, she was preoccupied with a feeling of hopes sinking. She woke at night primed for sounds in the dark, for the flapping of a moth's wings too close to her face or the screech of a late-night siren on the city streets. Her fear was odd and diffuse. She waited to hear her name on Michael's sleeping breath, or for a word to come to her, or a dream—a sign that the world was all right and it was all in her head. Michael would rise early and shave and head out into the morning and for a moment it seemed that everything was in order, as it should be, as it always had been.

'You could always have a child,' he said then.

She almost smiled at the release his words brought, as if they'd been banked up treacherously between them. Outside she heard the blackbird trill, like a plea, *Hear me, hear me…* over and over. He turned his face to her. 'Well?'

'I don't know. And stop bringing it up slyly, like that.'

She went back to her chair in the sun. She used to think that a child might return her to poetry. That what the poets had once granted her—those brief encounters with the sublime—a child might too. But she would read a poem and feel the approach of something terrible. Fear and sadness without cause. Still she would keep returning to the poem. And then, one day, it came to her: a child would do the same. She could not trust herself to love a child without obsession. She might raise a child brimming with fears. She might grow to fear the child itself.

She felt Michael move about inside. She closed her eyes. It was his name that had first drawn her. It had evoked tenderness in her. She knew of no Michael who was not a good man. In the early days they walked about the city, finding pubs and cafés in whose dark corners they would hunker down. In the evenings he cooked for her and she fell under his spell. She slipped off her sandals and raised her bare feet onto his lap and, still talking, he took them in his hands. His touch, his burn on her, consumed her. After they were married he'd come home from work and they'd open wine and he'd talk of his day, and they'd sit there in glorious union. She could never have too much of him. But then, when the wine wore off, a little fear would steal in and occupy her. She thought she would get all used up, and he would know this. She thought there would never be enough of her for him.

In the afternoon she sat in the cool bedroom. The cottage had thick white walls and cold slate floors, softened with scatter rugs. His question lingered in her head, and, unexpectedly, a memory pressed in, from a winter's evening in London a few years before. They had emerged out of the Underground onto the crowded street at Earl's Court, tired and thoughtful and separate after a day wandering in the city. A mist began to fall, softly, magically, making the orange lights and the whole street opaque. She stopped and gazed up at this strange, vaporous light and when she went to move, a sea of dark faces encircled her. They pressed closer, soundless, menacing. She opened her mouth to say something. She felt a hand rough on her breast. She wheeled around but she was penned in. She saw Michael's blue rain jacket up ahead. She called his name. The gang pressed tighter. They will kill me, she thought, they will drag me into that alley and rape me and kill me before he has turned around. But then he turned and took in the scene, and, wordlessly, beckoned to her. *Come on, come on.* She stepped to the right and the pack swarmed with her. *Come on, hurry up*, his eyes were saying. She stiffened her shoulders and pushed out through the ring of youths and up the street towards him. She thought he would open his arms. *What the hell was that?* he asked. She looked around for a lamppost, a ledge, a shop window to lean on.

She looked around the bedroom now. If she were ever pregnant he would distance himself from her in public. He would not be proud to declare his paternity, like other men, men who walk beside their slow, swollen wives and lay a hand on the small of their backs, to take the strain.

Late in the afternoon she strolled down the lane, running her fingers along the frilled edges of ferns. A yellow ESB van passed the gate and stopped a little further on. Four or five young men climbed out and began to unload large spools of cable and equipment from the van and then rolled the cable into a nearby field. She heard a rustling in the bushes, a bird hidden in its depths, and she turned and walked back to her chair and her book. When she looked up a while later an ESB man in a yellow helmet had begun the vertical ascent of a pole. Voices drifted across to her. Her book fell to the ground. Then Michael was beside her. He said, 'Hi.' His look held an appeal.

An engine started up and they turned their heads. The ESB van began to advance slowly on the lane beyond the hedge. A shout went up from the top of the pole. A cable attached to the climber's safety belt lifted into the air and grew taut. The van moved along, oblivious, dragging the cable until the pole began to lean sideways. Then a shout went up from below and she saw the climber drop, feet first, to the ground. Michael swore and began to run. She followed him down the lane out on to the road. She stepped up on the grass verge. The young men were bent over their fallen friend. They called his name, urgently. Seamus. Their accents were local, the clear clipped sounds of the north. Michael went into the field, looking like a man who could help.

'Don't move him. Keep talking to him.' She saw that the men were little more than boys. Their faces were pale and grave. She heard the clang of iron gates and running feet.

And then, miraculously, the fallen man stirred. The circle of comrades tightened, opened out briefly, then tightened again. She caught a glimpse of his head lifting slowly off the ground, as he emerged out of his strange remote world. His face came into view and raised itself to the sun.

Bob and Susan brought back trout and cooked it for dinner. They put on music and placed lighted candles on the table and the windowsill. Michael declined the wine, joking that he needed to keep his senses while those around him lost theirs. Outside the light was fading. They talked of travel and holidays and houses. Bob and Susan were hunting for an old brownstone in Chicago. They described exactly the kind they wanted. Romy excused herself and went out to the scullery. She ran the cold tap and stood looking out the window. She remembered the young ESB men's faces as their friend came to. She thought of them around his hospital bed at that moment, smiling, joking, changed. Saying his name over and over, as if they might glean something in its syllables, some hint of the marvellous.

Beyond the window a patch of rough ground led down to the sea. She watched lights flickering on the far peninsula. She did not know what she felt. She did not know what was coming. She thought that this couple, Susan and Bob, had somehow, inexplicably, brought misfortune down on top of them. She wanted to return to the way things were before. She crossed the kitchen and when she passed the table they were all laughing. In the bedroom Michael's shirt hung on the back of a chair. His briefcase stood packed and ready for the return to the city. She stared at the chrome clasps and then crossed the floor and flipped them open. She put a hand inside and urgently searched the slim fabric compartments.

A month before she had found something. He had been in the shower that day, preparing to leave for a big meeting with a client; he had been tense and harried all morning, liable to err. The briefcase was on the dining room table, packed and ready, then as now. His mobile phone began to ring inside, and, thinking the call vital, she leaned over and popped open the clasps. The phone rang off and she could not explain what had driven her to grope in the dark compartments as if seeking an answer to a question not yet formed. She found a brown envelope, and inside a passport-sized photo. A small boy with dark hair and a solemn face looked out at her. She turned the photo over and on the back, a name and a date, in blue ink: *Ross, b. 19 April 2004*. From inside the envelope, she drew out an acknowledgement slip with the letterhead of their city lawyer, and three words, handwritten in black: *All sorted, Tony*.

When she returned to the table Bob refilled her glass. He got up and announced that he was putting on Schubert. She knew before the approach of the first note that it would arc its way into her and with each successive note there would be an unravelling.

'A man almost died here today,' she blurted out, and they all turned to her.

'Oh, I knew there was something we had to tell you,' Michael said, seeking and then holding her look.

She watched his mouth move as he told the story. He paused every now and then to let her contribute but there was nothing she could add. Afterwards, Susan switched on the lamps. They were talking about European cities then. Bob and Susan argued gently over Venice, he insisting it was a crowded, overrated city for tourists, she pleading its history, its architecture, its light.

'What it had in the past has been lost,' Bob said. 'All that literary and artistic weight has pulled it down. Now it's just a bunch of beautiful empty buildings, gazing at their own reflection in the water.'

'It's a lovers' city,' Susan said, 'a bit like Paris in that respect. It's a city one must see with a lover.'

'I don't know,' Michael said. 'Romy and I fought all the time in Venice. I couldn't stand the heat and the crowds and the narrow alleys.' He met her eyes for an instant.

'We spent a lot of time complaining too, Susan, if I remember correctly,' Bob said.

'I think maybe the lover should be new,' Susan continued. 'You know that early stage when you know very little about each other... and it's all to play for and you're in a kind of glow.'

'Go on then,' Michael said. 'We're all ears.'

'No, it's nothing, really,' Susan said.

But he pleaded, mockingly, until she relented.

'It was before I met Bob, of course! Or Duncan! I had just arrived in Paris and I was waiting in line for a phone to try to book a room. There was a guy behind me, an American too, also looking for a hotel room. We got talking. He was twenty-eight, a doctor—handsome—on his first trip to Europe. Well, actually, he was getting over a divorce. Anyway we had no luck with the phone so we went to a small café where we found another phone and we each took turns calling around while the other one stayed with the luggage. Eventually I got a room—one room with three beds—so I took it, and I gave him the option of sharing. So we checked in and then went off to see the city and later we had dinner. And the next day we did the same and we… fell in love, I guess… People fall in love remarkably easily. He was a sweet guy. We were in a beautiful city… he made me feel safe. We were lovers for a week.'

In the lamplight she had grown seductive, and the story, slipping from her, added a new dimension, made her vulnerable. Her long slender neck reminded Romy of Picasso's gored horse that they'd seen in Barcelona—the beautiful white horse brought to its knees, the tip of a sword emerging from the ground, poised to pierce the pearl-white neck, spurt blood from the jugular.

'And then?' Michael asked, 'What happened then?'

'Oh, we had to say goodbye. He was going on to Rome and I had to return to the States.'

Nobody spoke for a while.

'I read some research recently,' Susan said then, 'that proved men are actually more prone to falling in love at first sight than women.'

In the candlelight Romy looked across at Michael. His eyes met hers and she felt herself surrender.

Later on they piled into the car and Michael drove them up the mountains. The road rose and they rounded bends and the headlights shone high in the trees, like searchlights. The radio was on low and a woman sang the blues. After a few minutes, without warning, Michael switched it off.

'Bob, are you drunk yet? Start us off on a song there.'

They laughed and argued and finally hit on a song. Romy looked out the window at the forest. All day long she had coasted on the brink of tears. She looked down to where the trees parted and a river flowed, and for an instant she saw a campfire in the clearing. Men and women and children were laughing and dancing, as if there was music there. The flames licked the trees and shadows leapt on the children's faces. She pressed her face to the glass. Her heart beat faster. Then the car climbed and rounded a bend and the fire and the dancers disappeared.

They emerged out of the forest onto a high moonlit road. She felt her mind remote. She thought that by now she would have had the key to him. She would like to be able to say things to him. To be able to say, *You are mine.* She would like to be a different woman, a strong strident wife, one who would reach into a briefcase and turn her face hard towards her man and say, *What's this, then?* She would like, for once, to shock him, shame him, shake that indifferent heart of his.

He reached across and took her hand. His face was lit by the dashboard. For a second his eyes were desolate. Had he loved that woman, that mother? Had he been wounded? Had he loved enough to wish her, Romy, dead?

The song ended and they started to descend. Bob asked a question and Michael answered. She listened to his voice. His words trailed out of him with strength and clarity and certainty and instantly it came to her. This is what he had carried for her— this is what he had afforded her. He had gone ahead of her and tested the world. He had verified it for her. Outside, the forest was bearing down on the car. Suddenly she felt doomed and everything run to ruin. Perhaps there is no key, she thought, perhaps there is no key to anyone, not even to ourselves, least of all to ourselves, to our own terrified hearts. The singing started up again and the words swirled around her. She longed to climb down into the forest, and walk in the river and succumb to the sound of water tumbling over ancient stones.

INSOMNIAC

It is Saturday evening and below his window Andrew's two daughters are playing Hospital with their friends. Occasionally he hears the whine of a siren and their pretend voices calling out orders. They rush around the garden tending to patients on trolleys. They race out of the house every day and rush headlong into these other roles.

His room is small and cramped. He has a large drawing board with compasses and squares and pencils lying in the well at the bottom. It takes up most of the space so that he is forced to the edge. Some nights he comes up here to work and he draws the curtains and switches on a lamp, throwing sharp light on the paper. Outside the street is always quiet, with the neighbours all enclosed behind walls. He sharpens his pencils—he is eager, optimistic, then. He rolls up his sleeves, his head teeming with ideas. Then at the very point of commencement he loses momentum and his plans slip from him and he stands looking down at the paper without a thought.

He opens the window and leans out to look at the girls. They have the garden hose out and when they see him, Rachel, the eldest, aims the jet of water up at him and they both squeal. He tells her to water the plants in the border. A neighbour up the street is mowing grass, over and back, starting and stopping. He thinks of the tiny spindles of grass flying out from the blades. Rachel is struggling with the hose. She is serious about her chores. He tells her to straighten the twist and when she does so the water shoots out at her sister. He likes to watch them. Sometimes he wishes they would fall over lightly so that he could comfort them. There is always some hesitation in him. Ann is easier with them, she knows what to do. When he drives into the street some evenings she is on the footpath dragging toys and bicycles and children back towards the house.

Ann comes out of the house now with Ian, fat and placid, in his pushchair. She is going to Saturday evening Mass. She looks up at him and squints. 'Do you want to come?'

He makes a doubtful face. 'What about the girls?'

'They'll come if you do. We'll only be half an hour.'

He shrugs and she says, 'Okay, Okay.' He watches her go out the drive and along the footpath. She is tall and slim and wears a green dress with small flowers, and white sandals, and, for a moment, there is nothing in her back that he recognises. She belongs to the street more than to him, to the milling and spilling of children and neighbours and gardens. She slows, checks her watch, then quickens her pace down the street.

He goes downstairs and takes a can of beer from the fridge and stands drinking it at the kitchen window. She has asked him to mow the grass. He will have to cross the garden and lift out the mower from the shed. He imagines revving it up and turning it onto the lawn, like an assault weapon. Unseen things, worms and snails, will be mown. He remembers the neighbour's grass and the thought of its dispersal grieves him. He goes into the living room and switches on the television and zaps it to mute. He glances at the clock on the mantelpiece every twenty or thirty seconds. In an hour or two the light will fade. He knows already—it is a feeling he gets—that tonight will be sleepless. It is worse in summer. The stillness of summer nights unnerves him. He fears he will stumble on something. He thinks he could sleep through a storm, that his sleeping self would sense the elements fully at play, fully occupied, leaving him free to fall into deep forgetful sleep. On quiet nights everything is singled out under the moonlight, and he sits ambushed and conspicuous in the middle of it all, and it is this visibility, this awareness, that causes his sleeplessness.

He lies on the couch and drifts off. He awakes to the sound of Ann's key in the front door and the girls' chatter in the hall. She will feed the children and put them to bed and then they will sit side by side on the couch and watch TV and eat supper in silence.

For over an hour he has lain awake listening to Ann's breathing. His thoughts are profuse tonight. There is expectation in his body. He gets up and goes into the study. He is reminded of Monday morning, the office, the endless cycle of work and home and long nights. It will go on and on. He goes downstairs to the living room and flicks through the TV channels. He finds a foreign film with subtitles. A man is walking along a beach at dusk. A boy on a horse passes him. The man walks to the end of the beach, then over rocks until he runs out of land.

He sits back with his arms folded across his chest. He remembers the dead horsefly on the windowsill of his study. He came upon it earlier, its legs in the air, its thin wafery wings lying flat. The heat of the sun will dry its body outright. He thought he could smell its deadness, and the smell of warm dust that never leaves that room. Some nights he thinks it's his own dust that he smells, that specks of him rest on the shelves and the windowsill and on the spines of books. He thinks that he is atomising particle by particle, and he is getting a preview of his own dissolution each night.

He lights a cigarette and inhales deeply. Before it is finished he flicks it into the fireplace and returns to the study. In the rooms around him Ann and the children sleep. He can hardly remember a time before this life, this house, this marriage. They have all toppled in on him. He remembers a moment from school years before. Something funny had made him laugh in science class and he could not stop and the teacher, a young woman named Pearl, grew angrier and angrier. The angrier she grew the more he laughed. And then, without warning, she raised the textbook she was holding and brought it down on his head. *Thwack, thwack, thwack.* And he laughed on. He looks around the office some days, at his colleagues, searching for telltale signs in them, of some slippage in their lives. There are days when he feels they are all watching him, waiting for the breach. He puts his head in his hands. Lately it has hit him. All new worlds of possibility have closed off, utterly. He fears a loss of faculties. He thinks he has already lost some foresight or insight. He knows it is happening and that he is beginning to shed, and that the dust particles are visible only to him.

'Andrew?' Ann is standing at the door.

She sits in the armchair opposite him.

'Why are you up?' he asks.

She shrugs and curls her feet up under her. Suddenly he likes having her there. A soft hope spreads over him. He has an image of the two of them at the kitchen table, talking, drinking tea, until the sun's rays break over the back wall.

'You need to see someone,' she says.

He shakes his head. 'More pills, more Prozac—no thanks!'

'You're worrying too much. Why are you worrying?' Her voice is full of mercy.

He looks at her and considers something. 'You remember Brian Sinnott? From the tennis club?'

She shakes her head and yawns.

'Pete knew him from way back. We used to play him and his friend sometimes, go for a drink afterwards. He was a bank manager in town. He was a nice guy—*is* a nice guy, he's married with a couple of kids. '

'What about him?'

'He lost his job.'

'God. What happened?'

'Fingers in the till.'

'You're joking!'

'The bank is going to take a case.'

'Jesus… Why do people do that? How old was he? What kind of guy?'

'Dead normal. Mid-forties. Just… flipped.'

'God… his poor wife.'

The landing light is shining into the room. Her skin is pale. She was always beautiful. He wonders what she thinks about, if she harbours secret thoughts, unspeakable yearnings.

'We should talk more,' she says.

'What d'you want to talk about?'

'I don't know… Tell me what you think about. Tell me what you do here at night.'

He presses the heels of his palms into his eyes.

'I work,' he says. 'Sometimes I read.' He glances at the bookshelf. 'I walk around the house and check the kids. Some nights I look at you.' She looks down at her hands. 'Other nights I leave the house, drive around.'

'You leave the house? At this hour?'

He nods.

An upstairs light goes on in the house opposite. He imagines an infant crying.

'One night I drove into town,' he says. 'It was a warm night last summer. I was so alert… I felt so alive driving out of the estate… It was a Saturday night, Sunday morning…' His voice is low. He is remembering the hum of the engine. 'There were girls in short summer dresses climbing into taxis. I kept driving. The city is different at night, bright, edgy… The buildings are watching… I drove along the south city streets… I was stopped at a red light… I felt something… I turned and this girl in the next lane was staring at me, you know, as if she'd been there all the time. At the next set of lights she was there again, the same stare. So I followed her. We raced each other to the next lights, and the next. She turned onto a side street and pulled up. I got out and the first thing she said was "I knew you'd follow me." She looked ordinary, in dark clothes. I stood looking down at her. I thought it was a very daring thing she had just done and I said so.'

He stops talking and looks at Ann. 'For me too… it was daring.'

Ann stares at him. *Who are you*? he thinks. *Who are you with that hard face*? And then, *I don't care who you are.*

'She was a cop, a detective in the Drugs Squad. She asked me into her flat but I didn't go. I didn't. I couldn't bear the thought of sitting at a kitchen table under a bright light. So we drove. She moved over and I sat in and drove her car out of the city, through the suburbs.'

He remembers her sitting in the passenger seat, their bodies almost touching, as if she were a wife beside a husband.

'I remember everything,' he says '—the taxis, the litter on the streets, the closed shutters, and then further out—the road narrowing, the hedgerows, the foothills… before we knew it we were climbing. I said we could go back if she wanted. I didn't want to frighten her. We skirted a forest… I thought of you and the children asleep here. I thought of the way you sleep, on your back, with your mouth open…

'We pulled over and looked down on the city. I could see the lights on the coast road out to Howth. We got out and walked to the summit. The moon was out. There were old ruins with beer cans and litter strewn on the ground. She said that kids came up there from the city for drug parties. It was strange… so bright and silent and eerie… Beautiful, too.

'I told her stuff, about you and the kids, and work. I don't know why I told her… except that she was there…'

He remembers the moment, their perfect stillness. He remembers what he told her. Fears, fantasies, mistakes. She listened, and nodded at times. Her eyes were dead. He talked like it was his last chance at speech, and that she knew this. These nights he thinks of her out there in the city, driving around in her dark clothes and emptied-out eyes.

'She drove the car back down to the city,' he says. 'The sky was lightening by then, the streets quieter. She drove past her own street towards the canal and then parked. We walked through a warren of narrow streets to a flats complex. There were old cars and junk lying around. She put on a dark hat—like a beret—and slipped her arm through mine. We went through an archway into an inner yard. There was a clothesline with children's clothes on it. Half the flats were boarded up, scrawled with graffiti. There was an atmosphere… like we were being watched. We climbed a stairs stinking of urine and there was a pale girl sitting on a step, smoking, strung out. A door opened then into some kind of service area on a landing and this huge unshaven guy with tattoos stood there looking out as we passed. On the third floor she took out a key and let us into a flat.

'She was working. She picked up an envelope from the floor inside the door and went into a back room. She was talking on her phone. When she caught my eye she kicked the door lightly to close it. In the yard below there was a vehicle, like an old milk float from years ago, driving in, and the sun was coming up. I was so weary. I kept thinking, I have to get out of here. I opened the door and hurried down the filthy stairs and through the quiet streets until I came to my car… When I got back here you were still fast asleep.'

Ann's face is white. Her chest is rising and falling. 'Did you kiss her or…?'

'No. No.'

'Did you see her again?' Her voice is hoarse.

'I saw her on Grafton Street—I think it was her—a few months ago.'

He stands up. 'It's cold… Are you cold?' he asks.

'What was her name?'

'Patty. Patricia, I suppose.' He puts a hand out to her.

She slaps it away. 'Shit, Andrew, why are you telling me this? What are you doing to us?'

He feels the breakage in her.

In a few hours the sky will lighten, the streetlights will fade. He pictures them at the kitchen table.

'When did you grow this cruel?' She is talking into the dark.

He wonders what time it is. He thinks of time like a small worm crawling across the earth. He opens his mouth and whispers 'Go back to bed.'

THE SEWING ROOM

Alice sits back and checks the clock. Half past five. She has been sewing all afternoon and she gets up now, goes to the kitchen and makes a pot of tea. She does not eat as there will be a meal later. In her mind she goes over the things she has made ready for the night—dress pressed, shoes polished, handbag and gloves resting on the dressing table. A slight worry persists that the gloves will seem a touch contrived. There will be a parish function later to mark her retirement as a primary schoolteacher. There has never been an occasion in her life in which she has been the centre of attention.

She finishes her tea and returns to the sewing room. Her dress hangs by the window and she stands to admire it. She is a small neat woman and dresses become her. It is straight and collarless, with three-quarter length tapered sleeves, in a light navy brocade, and it has taken three weeks to complete. It is her own design, simple and understated, and she is grateful for the kindness of navy.

In the seven years since her brother Manus's death she has taken to planning, sketching and sometimes creating her own designs. She buys her sketchbooks—with Japanese girls in silk kimonos on the covers—and HB pencils and black ink pens at the stationer's in Derry that she has frequented for thirty-five years, taking the

Lough Swilly bus to the city one Saturday in every month. With her purchases wrapped and a mildly glowing heart she walks down the street and sits in an alcove of a hotel where she orders lunch. She eats slowly, pencil in hand, and dreams up her designs, and can scarcely contain herself until she is back in her sewing room again.

The room runs the width of the house. She sits at the back window to draw, and sews at the front where the sewing machine is set on a wooden table perpendicular to the window and the inward flow of light. A dark mahogany wardrobe with a long mirror set into its door stands against the wall, bearing down on the room. She gives her designs names; 'Clara' is a straight, tailored suit with a short jacket and skirt which she imagines made up in black bouclé wool and jade buttons; 'New Moon' is a classic evening gown in midnight blue satin, overlaid with chiffon to create a hint of a shimmer. She imagines them on smart women on New York streets, or on ladies stepping out to the opera on a summer's evening in Boston.

She moves into the sewing room late in the evenings in a slightly heightened state of mind. She lays tracing paper on the fabric and marks the measurements. She carefully cuts around it, then takes the fabric onto her lap and tacks the pieces together with large white stitching. She crosses the room to the Singer sewing machine and sews in silence, with lamps on, eschewing the radio programmes of concerts and operas and music-hall melodies that Manus had loved. In this room, the silence has its own notes, plucked from the twilight outside and the stone walls and the murmurs of the sea. In the half light of evening she slips into reverie. Hours pass and she cannot account for them. She works into the night, feeling nothing of her body—not even her tired eyes, or the hands that cut and fold and sew. Then she looks up and out of the window at the moon and remembers herself, and the prospect of stepping out of this room or out of this house, ever, is almost too much to imagine. She thinks that it is only her memory and these nightly recalls that have any substance, and that everything else she has ever done—teaching the school children, caring for her mother, tending to this place or sewing these dresses—counts for almost nothing at all.

The school's board of management will send a car to collect her just before eight o'clock. She stands at the front window and surveys the area below. Every night a fishing boat or two traverses the bay and their lights bob and dip on the water, winking up at her on the hill.

She opens the door and stands in the garden. The smell of July is everywhere—heather, honeysuckle, the scent of yellow furze and the faint promise of night-scented stock. There is a spot down the lane where, year after year, she awaits the appearance of primroses, their pale yellow a salve to the eyes after the bleak winter—always the bleakest of winters here. They spring out of this unlovely ditch and though she knows it is absurd to imagine that a small wild flower might yield up some message, their appearance after such a long time bestows certainty, confirms the existence of real and material things, their constancy, their permanence.

Her eye is caught by something bright on the grass. It is a child's pink hairband, made of elasticated cotton, with a sequined butterfly at the centre. Its presence here is a mystery and she is suddenly thrown by it. She glances around. We are always being watched, the nuns said, by God or the angels or the dead. She raises her head. The small uninhabited island far out in the bay reclines like a giant on his back. Down below on the main road the school is part hidden by the hedgerow. Her eyes glide to a snug two-storey house a little further on. Once it was the first place her eyes sought when she opened the front door each morning. The first chimney she fixed upon as she walked down the hill to the school, waiting for the trail of grey smoke to rise into the sky, and know he was up. *They* were up. I would have knocked down that outhouse at the back, she thinks, if I'd been him, I'd have knocked it down and got a clear view out to sea.

She switches on the immersion water heater and rearranges the box of face powder, lipstick and perfume bottle on the dressing table. She removes her glasses and her shoes and eases herself down onto the pink eiderdown. Thoughts of the evening ahead unsettle her. Pupils, past and present, the local curate, the principal Con Gallagher, half the parish will be there. There will be a meal—a cold meat salad and desserts—prepared by the ladies of the parish, and then speeches and toasts and finally the presentation. She cannot stand to be looked at. She opens her eyes. This is my place, she thinks—this house, these rooms, contain me. She switches on the lamp by her side. It casts an orange glow on the walls. This had been her parents' room. She remembers evenings here, looking out the front window. She dates the start of her own conscious life to the moment when she was two, and, bathed in light, she saw for the first time the top of her head in the mirror of the wardrobe door. She tries to reimagine herself at two. She brings her hand to her face and presses on her eyelids, to stem the flow of tears.

There had been a child. His hair had grown from fair to dark in one year. His ears were small and, she thought then, a little too close to his head. He had learnt to walk at ten months. She'd come home from school through the city streets on winter evenings and the upstairs flat would be warm, with condensation running down the window panes, and Kathleen would hand him to her and his weight would sate the ache in her arms and there was nothing sweeter, ever, in her life after that. When he was born she thought of him as having come out of another realm, uncontaminated, pristine, whole. His eyes turned to the window, like a plant straining towards the light, and she wanted to say *no, no, stay pure.* She whispered—she dared not say it aloud—*my son.* She whispered his own name and his father's name into his ear. She almost forgot to eat. At night he slept beside her in the narrow bed set against the wall. She wanted nothing to divide them. At times she wanted to put him back inside her.

On Saturdays she walked around the city, pushing him in his pram, fearful of being sighted by the nuns from her school. She went out early to the library and to bookshops and to the Botanic Gardens, and one Saturday morning in spring she took a bus out of Belfast to Strangford Lough. The bus driver helped her with the pram and she held him on her lap for the journey, like any other mother. They passed a fishing-tackle shop on Lower Donegall Street, a strange shop with a dark interior that she walked past every day on her way to school. The surname was written in sturdy red lettering above the door. *Sweeney.* The sight of this name, with the child sitting there on her lap, gave her a bearing. She bent her head close to the child's and whispered the two syllables in his ear.

She was eighteen that summer and home from St Mary's Training College in Belfast. Neighbours worked together saving hay and turf, bending and sweating and labouring from dawn to dusk, the women returning to the houses at noon to bring out sandwiches and bottles of sweet tea. She worked side by side with Manus. With Hughie Sweeney and his younger brothers, too. Years later she came upon a print in a bookshop— it was a photograph of a young man and woman on a Paris street. The young man looked just like Hughie, shy and clumsy and lost. His tall, thin rangy body in baggy trousers and a pullover, his head lowered a little, and hands like Hughie's—big rural hands that he never knew what to do with. Hughie's voice was thick with the local accent and he had a habit of nodding a little too fervently as if he was still greeting the person long after meeting them. When she was alone with him the nod got worse. They started to fall in together at the work and in the comings and goings to the fields. He had a black and white sheepdog, Percy, who followed him everywhere and he told her of a neighbour who had never named his dog but whistled and called out *Dog* and the dog came, and they both laughed at his story.

That day in late August when the work was all done, they had gone up the mountain so that Hughie could fish from a small lake high up. He carried a homemade fishing rod and a jar of bait, and she, in her sleeveless dress, tucked a book from her college course under her arm. They walked along a stony lane that wound its way around the back of the mountain. Halfway up Percy stopped and looked back, uncertain, and Hughie told him to go on home. Wild goats perched high up on tiny rocky outcrops and she, afraid of heights, had to look away, for fear she might cause them to topple off. The path narrowed and the overgrown briars caught on her dress and he had to disentangle her. She felt her face flare red when he leaned behind her. At the top the mountain opened out to surprise them—a secret plateau of luxurious grass and heather and bog cotton, high and concealed and embedded into the summit. He told her the name of the place, *Áit na hAltaire*, the altar place, named after the secret Masses celebrated there in Penal times.

She would have preferred not to read, to talk instead. She grew hot and tense and could not follow her novel. She brushed off a fly and she saw he was looking at her and her heart rose. She turned back to her book, to its story set in nineteenth-century London society, and on this mountain on this bright day the characters and their lives felt dull and stifling and irritating. She left the book aside and got up and walked off to find a view of the sea, but there was none. The collar of her dress was stiff and hot against her neck. She lifted her hair to cool off. She listened out for birdsong. It is too far up, she thought, birds don't fly this high. She would have liked to open her arms out wide and run in circles under the sun and call out the name that was coursing through her head all summer.

146

Instead she pulled wisps of bog cotton and rolled them between her fingers and thought of slaves toiling in American cotton fields in the searing sun all day long.

She knelt down and touched small purple flowers that she had never seen before, and it seemed a shame to pull even one. When she looked up, Hughie's eyes were on her again and he smiled and something stirred and swelled and dropped inside her. She smiled back and felt suddenly drenched in his smile and in the light and the blueness of sky. She sat back and placed her palms firmly on the heather, to steady herself. He left down his fishing rod and turned to get bait from the jar. She kept her eyes on him, her chest rising and falling, her heart egging her on. She crept over the heather and leaned in and pounced on the rod and made off with it. He jumped up and ran after her, round and round. She moved fast, the rod high over her head, laughing. She ran through the heather and the long grass and around the lake's edge and then he caught her by the hem of her dress and brought her down. He was lying on top of her, breathless. The heather scratched her upper arms. The laughing stopped. His eyes were hazel, dappled with green. Speckled eyes, you have, like a speckled thrush, she thought. He searched her face, then stroked it with his finger. He lifted her hair and touched her neck and shoulders and she felt every part of her gather and rise to meet his touch. They pressed hard against each other, and his body frightened and delighted her. Her own wanton body ached and opened and every cell in her belly, in her womb, cried out for him and she could not have stopped it, she could not have stopped it.

Then it was over and he was lying in his white vest and open trousers on top of her. He pulled away but his face had darkened. After he had put on his shirt he looked down and saw that he had buttoned it wrong and a look of unbearable sadness came on him. They did not say anything and he went back to his fishing and she to her book, and she was filled with terror and shame at what had just happened. But then later, as they were leaving, he said, 'I'm going to get you a pup, for next summer,' and he took away some of her shame. She would have liked him to hold her hand or kiss her hair, or something, before they went back down the mountain.

She wrote to him in the fifth month—a letter full of apology and dread and small proffered hopes—and again in the seventh. She thought he would come. In the ninth month she sat her final exams and imagined that he had never got the letters. Her mother came to the city to talk to her. Her friend Kathleen Doran from Monaghan got her through it, and, afterwards when she got a teaching job, Kathleen and Kathleen's younger sister took turns minding the child.

It could have gone on like this. She could have lived in the city and raised him, and it would all have come right in the end. But her father fell ill and a job in the local school had her name on it and someone, somewhere—her mother maybe, or an aunt in America—thought that it all fitted, that it all made sense. And she was young and torn with doubt and guilt and duty. And on a wet Belfast evening in November, when he was eighteen months old, she handed the child into the arms of her mother's cousin, a childless woman in her forties, visiting from Boston. The husband, a tall handsome American, stood guiltily in the background. Legal papers followed a few weeks later. She went back to the flat that evening and cut off her long hair and walked the city streets that December under bright brutal skies, past gardens with bare trees whose beauty almost broke her, past people who gazed at her and could not have known what she knew, or felt what she felt. Her father died two months later and Hughie Sweeney began to walk out with Marie Gallagher and within three months she was back in the stone house set into the hill, the daughter, the teacher, the breadwinner. And that was that.

*

Her mother never spoke of it and Manus never knew. She saw the child everywhere—in the small boys who walked through the school door every September; in Manus's long straight back and serious face, in the elaborate wallpaper with the peacock which she and her mother hung in the sitting room and which would hang there for decades, a constant reminder of the visit to Belfast Zoo one Saturday and the peacock that had duly obliged and unfurled its feathers for the mother and child.

Once, ten years or so later, she confronted her mother. She remembers the moment: a winter's evening, Manus sitting at the table reading his library book, her mother sewing a button on a coat, the television on. Manus got up and went outside, the way he did some nights after reading, as if to recover from the contents of his book. Alice had been watching *Hawaii Five-O*. And Steve McGarrett, as he did every week close to the end, turned to his partner and with a wry contented smile, delivered his catchphrase, 'Book 'em, Danno,' and then turned and skipped down a flight of steps and disappeared off camera. And she saw the child in that instant, as she did every week, after every episode, saw him sitting with a father in a front room with a picture window bearing onto a lawn with sprinklers, and a mother making popcorn in a kitchen with wooden cabinets and a big fridge, and then the child getting up and turning to that father with a broad happy grin, and pointing a finger and calling out 'Book em, Danno,' and the two of them tipping and gripping and thumping each other as the credits rolled, all high fives and low slaps, all confidence, all American, and all she ever had to reimagine him, to re-envisage him, to cling to, every single day and night and week of this miserable life.

'Did she ever write?' she asked her mother that evening.

'Who? Did who ever write?'

'You know well who,' she said coldly. 'Was there ever a letter or a card or a photograph?'

'No.'

'Nothing? Ever?'

'Nothing.'

And then out of the blue, years later, a month before her mother died, a visiting American relative sitting in the kitchen one day said 'Ellen's son trained as a lawyer, you know. He qualified last year. He's with a big firm in Boston, I believe.'

She had been turning towards the sink to fill the kettle and all sounds dissolved behind her and then, to steady herself, she looked up and out and a long slender bird, like a heron, was flying past the window.

She had packed his things that morning and handed them over as if they had never been hers. She had written a long list of things that he liked and needed—how buttons, tags and cuffs made him itch, how he liked to touch the edge of his serge cotton blanket every day, every night, every moment, and look out the window first thing in the morning to check that the earth was still there—a list written and discarded and rewritten many times because it made her frantic and insane.

The couple had hired a car and were touring around Ireland. They did not want the pram. They sailed on a liner from Cobh. She thought there might be dolphins for him to watch. She thought of him on the deck of the ship scanning their faces for some trace of her, fingering the wool of his Fair Isle jumper, making concentric circles on his tummy with his index finger, as he looked out from a small, grave face. At the last minute before they left the flat he had pointed to a shiny green apple sitting on the dresser, and later she thought of this and saw significance in it, saw significance in everything. She had taken the apple and placed it in his hand and as they rode in the taxi he bit into it with his small new teeth and left little nibbled marks on the tough skin. Then, as they pulled up at their destination, he looked into her eyes for several seconds and silently, meekly, handed back the apple. This act remained with her forever. At the front door of the flat two nights later, feeling around inside her handbag for her keys, she touched the apple's cold skin. She unlocked the door and stood under the bare bulb in the kitchen and stared at the apple, at the little bites and teeth marks, and the current ran out of her, and she thought then that she would rather have had her head cut off.

From the window she can see the car snaking uphill and she breathes deeply and stands ready. The sea is shining in the evening light. She has a clear view of the parish hall and the church and, a little further on, closer to the water, the cemetery. Cars are parked along the road and people in bright summer clothes are moving towards the hall.

When his children, first one, then two, then four daughters, were born she had thought that when the time came she would not be able to teach them. She remembers a June day, years before, when she brought flowers to her father's grave and stood there trying to call up some memory of him, distracted by the sun gleaming on stone and sand and by the birds singing—one bird praising the day with the same two notes *ch-wut, ch-wut, ch-wut* over and over—and then others with their own chorus, *chwee, chwee, chwee*, and she trying to recall her father but nothing coming except the child, and the birdsong gradually growing louder and shriller as if all the notes were tumbling into disharmony and all the birds into disagreement until she could bear it no longer and ran from the grave.

But she had scarcely reached the path when there they were—a vision before her, like the holy family—coming over the stile. Hughie, lifting the smaller girl, then the bigger one, and finally, reaching out a hand to Marie, as she twisted her body, swollen with child, through the stile. She was wearing a green summer dress and flat white canvas shoes. Her arms were bare and freckled. The small children and small platitudes saved Alice. And Marie, open

151

and friendly and oblivious, so familiar, so at one with him by her side, that Alice had an image of their married life—of Marie washing and folding his shirts, his socks, his underthings, of nighttime and warm sheets and the smell of their bodies, of whispers, and shared physical things. And then Marie telling her that Imelda would be starting school in September, and then Imelda, with something wriggling in her arms, leaning forward and dropping it. A small black pup came tumbling towards Alice and sniffed her shoes and wagged its tail joyously. Marie smiled and Alice smiled too and looked down, and then he bent down suddenly, fiercely, and scooped up the pup, chastising it, and he cast his eyes briefly, shamefully, on hers. As he withdrew, his arm brushed against the swollen belly, and Marie placed a hand lightly on her stomach and looked up at him, a knowing look, and Alice saw it for what it was, saw what Marie was showing her, what all women in this state proudly, shamelessly, declare to the world: the potency of their men, their private married acts, their fecundity, their triumph. *This is what he has done to me, this big belly. This is his seed he has planted in me. This is his child I am bearing.*

She sits next to the driver as they bump down the lane and onto the main road. As they approach the hall she becomes agitated and asks him to drive on a little. They pass the hall and he turns off left towards the cemetery and the shore. He pulls over at the bridge, and says in a gentle voice that it can be hard, sometimes, to face people. She looks at him for a second, this local man with soft blue eyes, and she is moved with gratitude to him.

The priest and the principal receive her at the door and she is ushered into the hall where everyone is waiting. They stand and clap and she follows the two men to the top table. The microphone is switched on and the evening is announced. During the meal she nods and smiles and talks to those next to her. She knows all the words and all the answers that are required. She picks up her fork and brings food to her mouth. She feels the blood pulse through her temple. She closes her eyes for a second. *Oh, to be far from here.*

The parish committee presents her with a suite of crystal goblets and a wallet of notes and she is lauded for her work and dedication. She is handed the microphone and tremulous words issue from her mouth about the fine people and the beautiful children of the parish. The tables are tidied away and everyone wants to talk to her. She will miss the job, she tells them. It is the truth. She will miss seeing the new batch of infants every September, eager and expectant and glowing. She will miss listening to their first faltering attempts at reading, and watching their tense bunched-up fingers grip a pencil and start to write.

Grown men and women, whom she cannot place, take her hand and hold it and recount classroom tales that she cannot recall. She is sitting at the top of the hall, as if at an altar, receiving them, and they bow a little, genuflect almost, and then retreat. All evening she has held herself steady, and now, out of the blue, odd thoughts and images begin to encroach. She thinks of the pink hairband lying in the garden, and imagines it being carried there by some nocturnal animal while she slept. She thinks of boats edging out into the great Atlantic swell, nudging over waves in the dark and then anchoring, and the fishermen unspooling nets, with the hum of the ocean and the heavens in their ears. She thinks of a city street far away and houses with wooden porches and dark, damp crawl spaces underneath that would frighten a child. They lean down, these strangers, these overgrown children, and kiss her cheek now as if they know her, as if she is theirs, and as they straighten she looks at their faces, aghast, and for a moment she is far from this place, out in the ocean, cast alongside a big ship among dolphins and screeching gulls and desperate calls and cries and goodbyes. She would like to flee the hall now, or rise up to the rafters, to the dark shadows, to some quiet hiding place in her heart. *Give Mammy a birdie, I said that day, and you cackled and lowered your head to mine and*

we nuzzled noses and I kissed you on the lips and the face and the eyes,
my sweet delicious child.

She makes her way down the hall to the ladies' toilet at the far end, grateful for the chance to walk, stopping a few times when she is waylaid. Then, as she is about to enter, she feels a light touch on her elbow.

'Alice, how are you?' She turns and looks up at Hughie Sweeney. He puts out a hand and she stares, shocked, at the hand that takes hers and she cannot wait to snatch it back again. 'I just wanted to say, good luck, you know, and… well… to wish you all the best.'

She gathers herself. 'Oh, thanks, Hughie, thanks, but sure I'm not going anywhere.'

'I know that, I know that. Still… all the same…' For a moment she thinks he is going to say something terrible.

'How're all the family? Imelda and Helen?' she asks quickly. 'Their kids must be getting big now. And the twins!'

It had not been difficult to teach his girls at all. Imelda came in that first morning, the sweetest thing, with his eyes and his earnestness and his anxieties, and then Helen and later the twins, bright and polite and diligent. And one day, when Imelda was twenty and training to be a teacher herself, she stood at Alice's classroom door to request some book, this beautiful, dark-haired intelligent girl, and Alice thought, *You would have found me, you would have come looking, you would have trawled the ends of the earth and found me.*

'Oh, aye, Imelda's eldest is at university now and Helen's one is—God, I suppose, he'll be starting soon too. Helen herself gave up work for a few years to mind the smaller ones.'

'Ah, sure it's hard to do both.'

'Aye, it is.'

There was a time when she had hardened her heart towards him. When she had walked past him at the school gate or at the church door, with anger and resolve and pride in every stride. And let her back fix him firmly with blame.

They stand a little awkwardly now.

'Aye, that's the way,' he says then. She smiles and makes to move away. 'Things have changed a lot,' he continues, a little urgently. 'You'd have noticed that in the school too.'

She nods. 'I did… big changes, indeed, over the years.'

'Aye, for the better too, if you ask me,' he says and then nods, and two women squeeze past them and when she looks up again, he is still nodding. She is completely arrested by this and recognises in the lined face and the lock of grey hair that has fallen over his forehead the same uncertainty, the hesitancy, the faltering of the eighteen year old on the mountain that day. She stares at him now. In his bleak eyes, in his high furrowed brow she sees, for the first time, something of what he too must have endured at the bottom of the hill all these years—the permanent disquiet, the forfeiture. He had known the child's name; when it was all over she had written him the name and the destination, and how that name must have threaded its way through him, attaching itself and gnawing into him, so that in moments of anger or anguish—when he raised his voice to Imelda or Helen or to Marie, when he laid a stick on the back of a beast or kicked a stable door—was it to himself the wrath was aimed, to himself and his lonely secret, his awful privation?

'Aye, Alice, things have changed. If things were different… Aye… It's not the same at all today. The young are right now—they do what they like. They don't care what anyone else thinks, and they're right too… They'll have no regrets then.'

She is standing in the dark of the kitchen, her handbag dangling from her arm. A light is blinking out on the bay and down below her is a land full of dark shapes. Her heart is racing. She would like to stand at the shore and look into the ocean's depths and let the waves break over her bare feet and watch them turn and flow back out, to break on other shores. She thinks of her life, her whole existence, as a catastrophe. She drops her arm and the bag slides off and she thinks how everything has sprung from one moment, one deed—the insane beauty and shock of the flesh, the fire of the soul—with consequences that flowed out and touched and ruptured every minute and hour and day of her life ever since. That brought her to her own crime, her own awful act, on a Belfast street, the *relinquishment*. Greater than all that had gone before or would ever come after. Making her heart grow small, making extinct everything that was essential for a life. Was it all fated, she wonders? Was the desire fated? And the shame? And the crime— was the crime fated, too?

In the bedroom she switches on the lamp and sits on the edge of the bed. She searches for a word but there is none capable of containing what she feels. She narrows her eyes and a procession of words crosses her mind, like ticker tape, and then she feels its approach, the only word that is ample; it rises out of her in a voice she has never heard in these rooms, an exhalation, an utterance, a cry. *John*.

Tears fall on her hands. She hears the faint hiss of the lamp. She looks around at the walls. Eventually her heartbeat slows. There is no repose, there will be no repose, just the long wait in these rooms, and the sea sighing in the distance.

The author is grateful to the Arts Council of Ireland for its generous support.

READ ON FOR AN EXTRACT FROM

AS HEARD ON BBC RADIO 4 BOOK AT BEDTIME
WINNER OF THE IRISH BOOK AWARDS NOVEL OF THE YEAR 2014
SHORTLISTED FOR THE COSTA FIRST NOVEL AWARD 2014

Tess Lohan appears to be a quiet child. But within lies a heart of
fire. A fire that will propel her from her native Ireland into the
hurly-burly of 1960s New York. In this city she will face the twists of
a life graced with great beauty, but forever floating close to hazard.
Joyous and heart-breaking, *Academy Street* journeys through six
decades and one incredible story.

'Exceptional' *The Times*

'Packed with emotional intensity' *Sunday Times*

'With extraordinary devotion, Mary Costello brings to life a woman who
would otherwise have faded into oblivion' J.M. Coetzee

'I read this book from cover to cover in one night, unable to stop'
Maggie O'Farrell

'A powerful and emotional novel from one of literature's finest new
voices' John Boyne

'Brings to mind John Williams's resurrected masterpiece, *Stoner*'
Guardian

£8.99 ISBN 978 1 78211 420 8
£8.49 EBOOK ISBN 978 1 7821 1419 2

www.canongate.tv

1

IT IS EVENING and the window is open a little. There are voices in the hall, footsteps running up and down the stairs, then along the back corridor towards the kitchen. Now and then Tess hears the crunch of gravel outside, the sound of a bell as a bicycle is laid against the wall. Earlier a car drove up the avenue, into the yard, and horses and traps too, the horses whinnying as they were pulled up. She is sitting on the dining-room floor in her good dress and shoes. The sun is streaming in through the tall windows, the light falling on the floor, the sofa, the marble hearth. She holds her face up to feel its warmth.

For two days people have been coming and going and now there is something near. She wishes everyone would go home and let the house be quiet again. The summer is gone. Every day the leaves fall off the trees and blow down the avenue. She thinks of them blowing into the courtyard, past the coach house, under the stone arch. In the morning she had gone out to the orchard and stood inside the high wall.

It was cold then. The pear tree stood alone. She walked under the apple trees. She picked up a rotten yellow apple and, when she smelled it, it reminded her of the apple room and the apples laid out on newspapers on the floor, turning yellow.

She lies back on the rug and looks up at the pictures on the wallpaper. Adam and Eve in the Garden of Eden. Her mother told her the story. She picks out the colours – dark green, blue, red – and follows the ivy trailing all over the wallpaper, all around Adam and Eve. They are both naked except for a few leaves. Eve has a frightened look on her face. She has just spotted the serpent. A serpent is a snake, her mother said. The apple tree behind Eve is old and bent, like the ones in the orchard.

She feels something in the room. A whishing sound, and a little breeze rushes past her. She sits up, blinks. A blackbird has flown into the room. It flies around and around and she smiles, amazed, and opens her arms for it to come to her. It perches on the top of the china cabinet and watches her with one eye. Then it takes off again and comes to rest on the wooden pelmet above the curtains. It starts to peck at a spot on the wall. She holds her breath. She listens to the tap-tap of its beak, then a faint tearing sound and a little strip of wallpaper comes away and the bird with the little strip like a twig in its beak rises and circles and flies out the window. She looks after it, astonished.

The door opens and the head of her sister Claire appears. 'Is this where you are? *Tess!* Come on, hurry on!'

Something is about to happen. Her older sisters Evelyn

and Claire are home from boarding school. She loves Claire almost as much as her mother, or Captain the dog. More than she loves Evelyn, or Maeve her other sister, or even the baby. Equal to how she loves Mike Connolly, the workman.

The door opens again, and Claire holds out her hand urgently for Tess to come. There are people standing around the hall, waiting. The front door is wide open and outside there are more people. She can hear their feet crunching the gravel and the hum of low talk. She looks around at the faces of her aunts and cousins, her neighbours. Her teacher Mrs Snee is smiling at her. Claire pulls her close – they are standing next to Aunt Maud now – and squeezes her hand and bows her head. Suddenly she is frightened.

A shuffle on the upstairs landing and everyone goes quiet. Men's voices, half whispering but urgent, drift down from above. She thinks there must be a lot of people up there but when she looks up there are only shadows and shoulders beyond the banisters. She sighs. She will soon need to go to the bathroom. She looks down at her new shoes. She got them in Briggs' shop in the town during the school holidays, along with the green dress she is wearing. Her mother got new shoes that day too. And a new blue dress. Her mother bent down to tie her laces and Tess left her hand on her mother's head, on the soft hair.

The stairs sweep up and turn to the right and it is here on the turn, by the stained-glass window, that her uncle's back comes into view. Light is streaming in. Her heart starts to beat fast. She sees the back of a neighbour, Tommy Burns, and her other uncle, struggling. And then she understands.

At the exact moment she sees the coffin, she understands. It turns the corner and the sun hits it. The sun flows all over the coffin, turning the wood yellow and red and orange like the window, lighting it up, making it beautiful. The gold handles are shining. It is so beautiful, her heart swells and floods with the light. She closes her eyes. She can feel her mother near. Her mother is reaching out a hand, smiling at her. She can feel the touch of her mother's fingers on her face. Her mother is all hers – her face, her long hair, her mouth, they are all hers. Then someone coughs and she opens her eyes.

The men are almost at the bottom of the stairs and the coffin is tilted, heavy. She is afraid it will fall. Her father and her older brother Denis get behind it now, lifting, helping. She looks down, presses her toes against the soles of her shoes to keep her feet still. She wants to run up the last few steps and open the coffin and bring her mother out. She looks at the handles again, and at the little crosses on the top. She tries to count them. There is a big gold cross on the lid. Last night, when her cousin Kathleen took her up to bed, they passed her mother's room. The shutters were closed and candles were lit. There were people standing and sitting and leaning against the walls, neighbours, relations, all saying the Rosary. She dipped her head to see past the crowd. She could not see her mother. Just the dark wood of the wardrobe and the wash stand. And the mirror covered with a black cloth. And leaning up against the wall, against the pink roses of the wallpaper, the wooden lid with the gold cross, and the light of the candles dancing on it. They put the lid on over her mother. She looks up at Claire, about to speak, but Claire says 'Shh', and tightens her grip on Tess's hand. A silence falls on the hall. She turns and sees the big brass gong that she and Maeve play with sometimes by the wall. She wants to reach for the beater and hit the gong hard.

The coffin is crawling towards the front door. Then the men leave it down on two chairs, and rest for a minute. When they pick it up again everyone walks behind it and it passes through the open door, into the sun. On the gravel there is a black hearse and a thousand faces looking at them. The men bring the coffin to the back of the hearse and shove it in through the open door, like into a mouth. Maeve starts to cry and Claire goes to her.

Tess turns and sees Mike Connolly at the edge of the yard, with Captain the dog at his feet. He is holding his cap in his hand. She thinks he is crying. Everyone is crying, but she is not. She looks up and sees the blackbird on the laurel tree, eyeing her. *You robber*, she wants to shout, *you tore my mother's wallpaper, and now she's dead.* She looks past the white railings that run around the lawn, over the sloping fields and the quarry, far off to a clump of trees. Then the hearse door is shut and she gets a jolt. She looks around. She does not know what to do. The evening sun is blinding her. It is shining on everything, too bright, on the laurel tree and the lawn and the white railings, on the hearse and the gravel and the blackbird.

The hearse pulls away and people start walking behind it. Her uncle's car follows and then the horses and traps, and the neighbours, wheeling bicycles. Claire is beside her again, leaning into her face. 'You've to go into the house, Tess. You and Maeve, ye're to stay at home with Kathleen.'

Her cousin Kathleen takes her hand, leads herself and Maeve around to the side of the house, down the steps into the small yard. Before they reach the back door, Tess breaks away and runs back across the gravel, the lawn, off into the fields. On a small hill she stands and watches the hearse moving up the avenue, turning onto the main road. It moves along the stone wall that circles her father's land, the crowd and the horses and traps walking after it. Sometimes the trees or the wall block her view. But she watches, and waits, until the black roof of the hearse comes into view again, flashing in the sun. It slows and turns left onto Chapel Road, and the people follow, like dark shapes. Then they begin to disappear.

She stands still, watching until the last shape fades and she is alone. She is gone. Her mother is gone. She feels a little sick, dizzy from the huge sky above. She feels the ground falling away from under her – the grass and the field and the hill are all sliding away, until she is left high and dry on the top of a bare hill. Like the Blessed Virgin in the picture in the church when she is taken up into Heaven from the top of a mountain. Maybe she, Tess, is being taken up into Heaven this very minute. She can hardly breathe. She turns her face towards the low sun and closes her eyes and waits. *Please*. She waits for her mother's face to appear, a hand to reach out. She leans her whole body upwards, desperate for the sun to touch her, the wind to raise her, the sky to open, Heaven to pull her in.

When she opens her eyes she is still in her father's field, and there, a few feet away, are cattle, five or six, staring at her with big faces and sad eyes. The ground is under her feet again, the grass is green, nothing has changed. She looks around, frightened, ashamed. She starts running back towards the house. She runs into the yard, searches the barn, the coach house, the stables. She sticks her head into the dark musty potato house and calls out, 'Mike, Mike, are you there?' and waits and listens. Everywhere is silent. Soon it will be dark. She hears the sound of a motor in the distance. A car is coming down the avenue. She stands and waits for it to appear in the yard. Her heart is pounding. It is the hearse, she thinks, returning. With her mother sitting up in the front seat, smiling, and the coffin behind open, empty – a terrible mistake put right. They had come to the wrong house. They had come for the wrong woman – it was old Mrs Geraghty back in the village they should have taken.

But it is not the hearse that drives into the yard. It is Miss Tannian, the poultry instructress. She steps out of her car in a green tweed costume and patent shoes. And auburn hair, like Tess's mother's. The sky is pink and as she comes towards Tess the last of the sun lights her up from behind. She is speaking to Tess, saying, *I am sorry, I am so sorry.* Tess runs away from her, off along the edge of the yard, under the arch towards the orchard. The big iron gates are open and she runs in and stands in the shadows. The apple trees are dark, their low crooked branches like old women's skirts. Her eyes dart all over the place, along the four high walls. And then she sees him, Mike Connolly, sitting on an old stump at the far end, his head down, Captain beside him. As soon as she sees him the tears come. She runs and falls at his feet and begins to sob.

CANON‖GATE.tv

CHANNELLING GREAT CONTENT

WATCH

INTERVIEWS, TRAILERS, ANIMATIONS, READINGS, GIGS

LISTEN

AUDIO BOOKS, PODCASTS, MUSIC, PLAYLISTS

READ

CHAPTERS, EXCERPTS, SNEAK PEEKS, RECOMMENDATIONS

DISCOVER

BLOGS, EVENTS, NEWS, CREATIVE PARTNERS

SHOP

LIMITED EDITIONS, BUNDLES, SECRET SALES